CLASH OF THE CRYPTIDS

PART 1

A NICOLE BERETTI THRILLER

LUKA T. JACOBS

Adam, thank you for your support,
company, and laughs.

FROM THE AUTHOR

Dear fearless readers,

Thank you for joining me for the third installment in the *Nicole Beretti Thriller* series. *Clash of the Cryptids* is a special one, told in two parts with Part 2 releasing shortly after this.

Part 1 unfolds in three layers: a brutal war between Dogmen and Sasquatch, Beretti's reluctant return to a hometown she tried to forget, and the slow unraveling of long-buried truths she can no longer outrun. It's a cryptid thriller at its core, but one rooted in memory, loyalty and reckoning with the past.

I hope you enjoy reading it as much as I enjoyed writing it.

Happy reading,

Luka T. Jacobs

CONTENTS

PROLOGUE

Deborah Gales turned off the highway and followed the narrow gravel road that led to Evergreen River Campground. The trees grew thicker as she drove, rising tall and dark on either side. A wooden sign appeared around the bend, weathered but legible. Eager to find a suitable campsite, she turned and followed the loop.

She picked a quiet spot near the back of the campground. It was bordered by trees on one side and backed onto a dense stand of timber. A bit uneven, but nothing she couldn't work with.

She sat for a moment in the driver's seat, breathing in the quiet. Then she smiled.

Her eyes drifted to the bobblehead figure on her dash, a tiny raccoon in a park ranger hat, still nodding from the bumps in the road.

"This will do," she said to it.

The raccoon kept bobbing.

She nodded back like they had an understanding.

This was what she worked for. Not the job itself, but the freedom it gave her.

The clinic contract up in Oregon had ended two days ago, and instead of heading straight south to her next one in Chico, she had decided to take her time. Traveling as a nurse let her move between places, shift through people and towns without having to stick anywhere too long. No apartment leases. No office politics. Just her, her camper, and the open road.

She climbed out and stretched. The air smelled good. Clean. Crisp enough to bite the tip of her nose.

Stillness settled around her. The air carried the dry, earthy bite of old leaves and sap, with a cool undertone like river stone. Afternoon light filtered through the trees in quiet, shifting bands. Her RV, a compact Class B, fit perfectly in the space. Just enough room for one, with everything she needed and nothing she didn't.

She pulled a couple of leveling blocks from the side

compartment and tucked them under the wheels, then tested the sway inside. Solid enough for the night.

The site was basic. A dented picnic table. A rusty fire ring. A patch of dirt just wide enough to park on. It suited her just fine.

Across the loop from her, she'd noticed another RV with bikes left out nearby. Quiet campers. No music. No kids. Just the faint smell of wood smoke and a couple of folding chairs left out.

She set up her small camp stove on the table and boiled pasta. Pesto from a jar. A sparkling water on the side. Simple. Comforting.

She ate in her folding chair with a book resting on her lap, though she barely turned a page. Her attention drifted to the tree line, then to the clouds thinning overhead.

Partway through dinner, someone stepped out from the other site. She gave a polite wave. The person returned it without a word. That was all the interaction she needed.

After cleaning up, she stepped back into the RV, closed the door behind her, and locked it.

By nine o'clock, she was tucked under a blanket in bed

with a steaming mug of tea on the small shelf beside her and her favorite true crime podcast playing softly in her ears. The voice of the host was calm and methodical. A case about a couple in the Midwest. Gruesome, but oddly relaxing in its familiarity.

She felt something bump the RV.

It wasn't loud. Just a soft jolt that made the frame rock slightly on its leveling blocks.

Her eyes opened.

She paused the podcast and pulled one earbud out.

Silence.

She stayed perfectly still and listened.

After a few seconds, she shook her head and exhaled quietly.

This is exactly why I shouldn't listen to crime podcasts at night. Now I'm jumpy over nothing.

A slow tapping started at the window near the door.

Three taps. A pause. Then another two.

It wasn't random. It seemed... controlled.

What the...

Her body tensed.

Could be a drunk. A curious camper. Someone thinking they were funny. She hated that it wasn't even an unfamiliar possibility. She had dealt with creeps before. Being a woman traveling alone always carried that risk.

She didn't move. Anxiety started to creep in.

The tapping stopped.

A second later, the door handle rattled.

Oh no.

Her pulse spiked. The handle jiggled again, harder this time. Then came a dull thud as something pushed against the door.

I locked it. I'm sure I locked it.

It held, but the whole RV trembled slightly from the effort.

She clutched the blanket tight, staring at the door. Her

pepper spray was in a drawer by the kitchenette. Her phone sat on the shelf beside her. Both felt like they were a mile away.

Please go away.

The jiggling stopped.

She stayed still, listening, eyes locked on the wall as heavy footsteps crept past just outside.

Slowly, she turned her head toward the narrow window at the foot of her bed.

A shape passed in front of it.

Oh my God!

Upright. Broad shoulders. Tall.

The head was massive.

Long snout. Pointed ears pulled back. The shape of a wolf, but walking like a man.

Her hand covered her mouth as instinct took over.

No freakin' way.

Her mind scrambled to make sense of it. A mask. A prank.

Some horrible joke. Maybe someone in costume.

But it hadn't moved like a person. It had glided. Like it didn't care who saw it.

You're just seeing things.

She stared at the ceiling, willing herself not to move. Not to make a sound. She strained her ears.

Nothing.

She started to think maybe it had moved on. Maybe she had imagined it or at least exaggerated what she saw.

Maybe it was just a man.

A man would be bad enough.

It's ok. It's gone. It's gone.

She counted slowly in her head. Ten seconds. Twenty. Thirty.

Still no sound.

Her muscles began to loosen. A little.

A slow, wet breath exhaled against the wall beside her head.

She squeezed her eyes shut.

Oh God.

It was so close she could feel the vibration of the air on the wall. It had lungs. Big ones. That wasn't her imagination.

A growl came next. Low. Too low to be human. The kind of sound you feel more than hear.

And then it started making a sound like it was grinding its teeth.

It was quiet at first. Subtle. A slow scrape like enamel against enamel. The sound of pressure. It reminded her of someone chewing their own tongue in frustration. Or restraint.

Please go away. Just go away.

The grinding went on for nearly a minute.

Her eyes burned from not blinking. She thought her chest might explode from holding her breath. Every instinct screamed for her to run. To grab something. To do something.

But she didn't move.

The roof groaned above her as something landed on it.

The whole camper rocked.

It doesn't know I'm here. It can't know.

Then came the scraping of claws. Metal on metal. Slow, dragging crawls. It moved in loose circles above her, each movement twitching across the roof like something testing its own patience.

It was crawling. Not stepping.

She imagined it crouched above her, tilting its head, deciding whether to rip its way in.

Please leave. Please go. Please.

She could feel her legs trembling under the blanket. Her fingers were numb. Her body wanted to run, but the animal part of her brain told her to stay down. Stay quiet. Hide.

A man's voice shouted outside. Close but not right next to her.

"HOLY SHIT!"

A heavy scrape came first, the sound of something sliding down the side of the camper. Then a thud as it hit the ground.

For a moment, silence. Then fast, retreating footsteps pounded away from her RV, fading into the trees.

Her heartbeat filled the space where the scraping had been.

It took time before the pounding eased.

Oh thank you God. Thank you.

And then she heard voices. Not one. Several. People speaking quickly, overlapping. Excited. Alarmed.

She could barely make out the words. She didn't try to.

She stayed where she was, beneath the blanket, curled into herself with wide, unblinking eyes.

CHAPTER 1

Special Agent Nicole Beretti moved through the compound quietly. Tactical units trained across the grounds. Coordinated drills, live-fire accuracy tests, and controlled breach scenarios unfolded in tight formation. The clipped calls of instructors echoed across the training yard. The air smelled like sweat and spent brass.

It had been months since she'd walked these grounds, but she didn't linger on it. She had come to speak with her boss, and that was all that mattered.

She and Special Agent Noah Jacobi had just come off a brutal case in Maine. A Dogman spirit had taken hold of a child's bedroom, tethered to the physical creature stalking the woods outside. They were trapped inside through a relentless snowstorm, forced to wait it out while the creature taunted them from the shadows. When the weather finally broke, they gave chase into the woods. Jacobi rushed in before she gave the word. He got lucky.

He often did.

Nicole didn't trust luck. She trusted strategy, timing, and knowing exactly where everyone was when it all went wrong.

Inside the Apex Jaegers division wing, the tone shifted. The noise of the yard gave way to the low pulse of servers and the dry whisper of filtered air. Monitors tracked movement across cryptid zones throughout the country. Analysts moved between mission control rooms, quiet and focused.

Nicole walked past them without pause and turned toward the corner office that oversaw it all.

Assistant Special Agent in Charge Nathan Ward, known across the division as ASIC Ward, was already on his feet when she entered.

He wore a dark gray suit, tailored but unadorned. Wire-rimmed glasses rested on his nose, and his salt-and-pepper hair was cropped short. At 56, he carried himself with the calm authority of someone who had earned his way into command. A long military career had shaped him well before he ever sat behind a desk. He'd held the position for fifteen years, long enough to see patterns most people missed. His expression was unreadable, as always. He motioned to the chair across from his desk.

"Agent Beretti."

She nodded once and sat.

"You got a call," he said.

"Yes, sir," Nicole replied. "From my uncle. Benjamin Beretti. He lives in Blackridge, CA, a few miles from the old property. He said he didn't want to bother me, but something's wrong."

Ward waited for her to continue.

"Started with livestock going missing. Now people. Two teens attacked, one lost a leg. Wolf-like creature mentioned. My uncle thinks it is Dogman-related. Possibly more than one."

Ward sat back slightly.

"That region's had Sasquatch presence for years."

"They're still there," she said. "They've never been overly aggressive with locals. This doesn't fit their patterns."

Ward dipped his chin. "You haven't been back to the house since the accident."

"I've visited the town," Nicole said. "Seen my uncle. But I haven't set foot in the farmhouse since the day before it happened."

Ward studied her for a moment. She didn't give him anything to read.

"You alright going back?"

"I can handle it."

He made a note on his tablet, then looked up again.

"You'll take Jacobi. The Maine job was handled clean, even with the rough ending."

"We've got a good rhythm," Nicole said.

"Any concerns?"

"He moves fast. Sometimes too fast. I've talked to him about it. Reminded him we're a team, not freelancers."

Ward recorded the note and moved on.

"We're expanding the Apex Jaegers," he said. "We lost an

operator in Utah two months ago. Replacement process is slow, but you and Jacobi are flagged as stable assets. If things stay solid, you'll stay paired. Long term, there's leadership potential here. Command is watching."

Nicole acknowledged with a glance. "Understood."

Ward leaned forward slightly.

"If Dogmen are crossing into Sasquatch territory, that's not an isolated threat. That's a challenge. I want full intel. Movement patterns, proximity to town, any signs of territorial displacement. Everything."

"You'll have it."

Ward stood. Nicole followed.

"I don't like sending you into something this personal," he said. "There are ghosts there, Nicole."

Her eyes stayed on his.

"The past has a way of following you, sir. I've made peace with that."

Ward gave a quiet look of understanding.

Nicole answered with a brief motion, then turned and

walked out.

Beretti stepped outside. The sky hung low, colorless and unmoving, and the air had that certain stillness that came right before snow. Wind threaded between the buildings, quick and biting, slipping beneath her collar. She pulled her jacket tighter and headed for the lot.

"Beretti."

She didn't need to turn to recognize the voice. Special Agent Kade Overley fell in beside her, too casual for someone who had clearly been waiting.

"Figured I'd see you around. Word gets around fast."

"I'm not here long," she said.

"Yeah, I heard. You and Jacobi, chasing monsters, getting noticed by the higher ups. Must be nice."

She said nothing.

"How's he doing, anyway? Still riding your coattails, or did they finally give him a leash of his own?"

Beretti kept her pace steady. "He's doing fine."

Overley laughed under his breath. "Sure he is. That guy

could walk blindfolded into a briefing and still come out with a commendation."

She stopped then, just long enough to look at him. Her tone stayed even.

"Jacobi puts in the work. Every time."

Overley held her gaze a beat longer than necessary, then looked away like it hadn't mattered.

"Relax, Beretti. Just messing around."

She turned and kept walking.

He hesitated, then called after her. "You know, if you're ever in town longer... maybe we grab dinner? Catch up properly?"

She didn't turn. Didn't answer.

By the time she reached her truck, the only footsteps she heard were her own.

Next stop: Blackridge, California.

Back to where it all started.

CHAPTER 2

FBI Special Agent Noah Jacobi leaned back in his seat and let out a contented sigh. "You know, I could get used to this."

Nicole Beretti didn't look up from her coffee. "You say that every time."

He swept his hand toward the sleek interior of the private plane. "Still true every time. No toddlers kicking the back of my seat, no line at security, and the pretzels don't taste like packing foam."

She allowed the faintest smile.

The Bureau had put them on a private flight that morning, moving fast after the call came in. An encounter with a wolf-life creature at a campground outside Blackridge. A witness had seen something. Not someone, something. It was enough for APEX to get airborne.

Jacobi stared out the window for a beat before turning his head. "So. Blackridge. That's your old turf, yeah?"

Beretti nodded. "Grew up on a small farm just outside town."

He sat up a little straighter. "Okay, refresh my memory. How old were you when you first learned about Sasquatch? I mean really learned. You've mentioned it before, but I've got a lot of high-priority nonsense rattling around up here." He tapped the side of his head.

Beretti raised an eyebrow. "Six."

His brow rose. "That young?"

"I'd seen them before that. They'd come through the field sometimes. I just thought they were animals. Just like deer or bears."

"And then?"

She shifted in her seat. "One of them tried to lure me into the woods. I didn't realize that's what it was doing. I thought it was just curious. It stayed near the trees, stared for a while, and every time I glanced away, it had moved further into the forest. Not fast. Just far enough to make me want to follow."

Jacobi sat forward. "Did you?"

"No. A voice in my head said not to. My mom was watching from the kitchen window and that night, she sat me down and told me what they were."

Jacobi's voice lowered. "What did she say?"

"As far as I can remember, she told me not to trust them. Ever. She said they weren't just animals. That they were something old, something that knew how to watch. And wait."

Jacobi leaned forward slightly. "That's intense for a six-year-old."

"She made sure it stuck, I guess."

They rode in silence after that, except for the steady crunch of pretzels from Jacobi's seat. Outside the window, Redding drew closer. Mountains framed the north, streaked with lingering snow and dotted with tall pine.

****

They landed just before noon at Redding Regional. The terminal was small, tucked beside open lots and a private hangar. No crowds, no announcements. It was all movement and silence.

The government-issued SUV was waiting when they landed. Soon after, they were headed northeast on a two-lane highway. Blackridge sat about ninety minutes out, past the tree line and into the colder edges of the valley.

Jacobi tapped the GPS screen. "Says we'll hit town by about one thirty."

Beretti kept her eyes on the road.

"You still have family out here, right?" he asked.

"My uncle. Benjamin. Everyone calls him Ben. He lives in town with his partner, Leona. They've been together twelve years."

"Close?"

"I visit once a year. I stay with them when I do. You will, too."

Jacobi looked out the window at the passing trees. "He the one who called this in?"

"He's the reason I requested the assignment."

He nodded. "What's he like?"

"A people person. Charismatic. Knows everyone. He's the kind of guy who'll stop to fix someone's fence just because he noticed it leaning."

"Sounds like a good man."

"He is."

Jacobi paused. "Any kids?"

"No. He was married once. The marriage lasted about five years."

"What happened?"

"She struggled with serious mental health issues. He told me he didn't fully see it at first, but the signs were there. He stayed with her, tried to support her, but it got worse."

Jacobi's expression softened. "She passed?"

"By her own hand."

Jacobi exhaled. "I'm sorry."

Beretti dipped her head briefly. "During the marriage, he

decided not to have kids. Said he couldn't bring a child into the world knowing they might inherit what she carried. After she died, he never tried again."

Jacobi looked at her carefully. "That's a hard choice to live with."

"He made it without hesitation. Besides, he ended up with me. I am sure that was more than enough trouble."

They drove in silence for a stretch, winding through pine-covered hills and past long gravel driveways. Fences lined the road, sagging between rusted posts.

Jacobi turned his attention back to her. "What was it like growing up out there?"

Beretti took a deep breath before speaking. "Quiet. Isolated. But not in a bad way. My mom gardened. My dad rebuilt old engines when he was home. He served in the military, so he wasn't always around. But when he was, he taught me how to handle myself. In the woods. With guns. How to pay attention to what didn't belong. And when he wasn't there, my uncle stepped in. He made sure I didn't grow up helpless. I was an only child so I guess I received all the attention."

Jacobi smiled faintly. "Sounds like you had more training

by ten than most agents have at twenty-five."

Beretti replied, "What I appreciated most was that I wasn't treated like I'd break. My father and uncle taught me everything they would've taught a son. And from my mother, I got the nurturing side."

Jacobi studied her a moment, then leaned back and rested his head against the seat.

"You kinda talk about them like you're reading off a personnel file. Like you disconnect when you talk about home."

Beretti glanced at him, then looked out the window.

She didn't respond.

Jacobi let it go.

****

An hour later, the GPS chimed as they passed a faded sign that read **Welcome to Blackridge – Est. 1867**. The paint was cracked. Someone had carved a heart into the wood and crossed it out.

Blackridge looked like a town that had held on to its identity without trying too hard. A few modern touches stood out. A new café sign here, fresh paint on a storefront there. But most of it felt rooted. The gas station looked like it had been built in the early 1900s, with narrow windows and a hand-painted sign that had faded to soft grays and blues. An old pharmacy, brick-fronted and squat, still bore its weathered mural of the mountain range, chipped but unmistakable. Nothing flashy. Nothing forced. Just lived in.

Jacobi looked out the window, wide-eyed. "You weren't kidding. This place is stuck in time."

"It never needed to change," Beretti said.

He watched as they passed a row of old mailboxes. A woman walked a dog along the gravel shoulder. A pair of kids rode bikes near the edge of a slow-moving creek.

Then the street narrowed and dipped, heading towards the outskirts of town.

They didn't speak for the last few minutes of the drive.

CHAPTER 3

The SUV rolled into the front loop of Evergreen River Campground. A line of county cruisers sat parked in the clearing, their light bars quiet. Deputies moved between two campsites near the back of the lot, speaking quietly.

The air smelled clean, pine swaying gently overhead as sunlight filtered through the branches in scattered beams. Birds chirped lazily. A couple of squirrels darted across the road, undisturbed.

The place looked peaceful, but Beretti and Jacobi knew better.

Beretti stepped out of the SUV and closed the door quietly behind her. Her eyes swept the area, adjusting to the stillness. The scent of crushed needles and faint ash lingered near the clearing, but otherwise, the campground looked ordinary.

Too ordinary.

Behind her, Jacobi got out and rounded the front of the vehicle, glancing around.

"Hard to believe this is it. So beautiful."

"In the daylight, it always looks like nothing happened," Beretti said.

A man stepped away from a small cluster of deputies and made his way across the grass toward them. Tall and solidly built, he wore a tan shirt and dark jeans. A gold sheriff's badge caught the sunlight on his chest. His boots were dusty, his gait relaxed but confident. The mustache and dark brown hair curling from under his hat were unmistakable.

Beretti didn't need to see his face to know who it was.

"Good to see you, kiddo," he said, pulling her into a warm, familiar hug.

"Hi, lo zio," she said.

She turned and gestured to Jacobi. "This is Special Agent Noah Jacobi. Jacobi, this is Blackridge's sheriff, Benjamin Beretti."

Jacobi blinked. "Sheriff Beretti? Wait... Beretti?"

Ben offered a handshake, smiling. "Uncle. Don't hold it against her."

Jacobi took the hand, still catching up. "Right. Makes sense now," flashing Beretti a playful stare.

Ben gestured for them to follow. "Come on. I'll walk you through what we've got."

They ducked beneath the crime scene tape and entered the main campsite.

As they walked, Jacobi leaned in slightly. "You didn't mention he was sheriff."

"You didn't ask," Beretti quipped.

Ben led them forward through the space. "We got a call just before midnight. Woman in a camper near the back reported strange noises. Said something was trying to get into her RV."

Beretti nodded slowly. "Deborah Gales, aged forty-four."

Ben confirmed it with a glance. "Yeah. Traveling nurse. Pulled in yesterday afternoon, parked alone. She had dinner outside, then went in and locked up. Everything was quiet until she said something bumped the RV. Then tapping on the window. When the door handle started to rattle, she knew something was wrong."

Jacobi looked toward the neighboring campsite. "Did she see anything?"

"She didn't get a clear look. Just a silhouette. Tall, upright, hairy, with a snout and pointed ears. She said it walked past her window, breathed against the side of the RV, then started crawling on the roof."

Beretti's expression darkened. "Crawling?"

"Yes. Circled above her. Then she heard a voice outside shout, and the weight suddenly shifted. She heard it slide down the side of the RV and then run off."

Jacobi nodded slowly. "And who was the one who shouted?"

Ben flipped through his notes, then paused. "Ash McMillan. He and a few friends were in their camper across from Deborah. He stepped out with his buddies for a smoke and saw it on her roof. Thought at first it was a bear until he focused on it. That's when he yelled."

Beretti raised a brow. "He got a good look?"

"Better than most," Ben said. "And here's the kicker... he's a cryptid enthusiast. Been following sightings for years. Said the second he realized it wasn't a bear, he knew what it was. Called it a Dogman."

Jacobi tilted his head. "Seriously?"

Ben gave a small shrug. "Yeah. Apparently runs a cryptid podcast. Said he always wanted to see one, but now that he has... he kind of wishes he hadn't."

Jacobi looked toward the treeline. "Tracks?"

Ben acknowledged with a dip of his chin. "We found some around Deborah's RV. Deep. Barefoot. Spread wide. We cast a few. The trail cuts off maybe twenty yards in."

Beretti crouched near a patch of flattened dirt and pine needles. "So it made sure it was seen. Left no damage. No death."

"But it left a mark," Ben said. "Deborah's still shaken. She barely slept. Ash is jittery. His friends want to leave town."

Jacobi folded his arms. "This Dogman wasn't shy. It definitely wanted attention."

Beretti stood. "And now it has it."

Ben pointed back toward the cluster of vehicles. "Ash and his group are over by the ranger's shed. They're waiting to speak with someone."

Beretti gave a short nod and turned toward Jacobi.

"Let's go talk to them."

The two stepped away from the tape, leaving the quiet campground behind as they crossed the grass toward the waiting group.

CHAPTER 4

They reached the SUV parked near the ranger's shed. Three young men lingered around it, their conversation low and scattered. One leaned against the side panel, arms crossed. Another sat hunched on the tailgate, chewing his thumb. The third stepped forward quickly when he saw them coming.

He wore a flannel shirt unbuttoned over a faded cryptid-themed tee and a ball cap that had seen better days. His posture was tight, and his energy buzzed under the surface like it didn't know where to go. His eyes were wide and tired, like he was still trying to convince himself what he'd seen had really happened.

"You must be the agents," he said. "I'm Ash. Ash McMillan."

Beretti took his hand first. "Agent Beretti. This is Agent

Jacobi."

Ash shook both their hands with quick, damp palms. "Didn't think I'd ever be saying this stuff out loud. Let alone to the FBI."

Jacobi's voice was steady. "Start wherever you can. We're listening."

Ash rubbed his hands down the front of his jeans. "We pulled in yesterday afternoon. Me and my buddies. Road-tripping across a few states, camping, filming stuff for this little cryptid channel I run. Mostly harmless. Dumb stories and gear reviews."

Beretti gave a nod to keep him going.

Ash glanced at his friends, then looked back at the agents. "We'd just finished dinner. Burgers. A couple beers, yeah, but we weren't drunk. We stepped outside for a smoke before bed, ya know?"

He paused and stared across the loop toward the RV. "I saw movement. Just out of the corner of my eye. I turned, and there was something on the roof of that camper."

He pointed directly at it.

"It wasn't a shadow. It was there. Huge. Low to the roof like it was crawling. My brain tried to tell me bear at first, but it wasn't. Ain't no bear looks like that."

His voice thinned as he spoke. "Its eyes were glowing. Not lit up from a flashlight or anything. Just glowing on their own. Red, but deeper. Almost amber. Like hot coals that were just starting to dim."

Jacobi stayed quiet.

Ash's hands trembled slightly as he tucked them into his sleeves. "It had a long body. Bent legs like dogs have. Dark hair all over but patchy in some parts. It had big hands, not claws."

Beretti asked quietly, "What did the face look like?"

Ash blinked, and for a moment his eyes glazed as if he was still seeing it. "Like something half-made. The snout was long. Teeth... God, the teeth looked too big for the mouth. Imagine a cross between a hyena maybe, a dire wolf, and a deformed German Shepherd. It was evil-looking alright."

Beretti asked gently, "What did it do?"

Ash swallowed. "It didn't move for a second. Just stared. I yelled. I couldn't help it. It was loud, instinct. As soon as I did, it slinked down the side of the camper and took off. Fast.

Right into the woods over there."

One of the guys on the tailgate finally spoke. His voice was flat but shook just a little. "We heard him yell and looked up. Thought he was messing around until we saw it on the ground, then bolt. Never seen anything move that fast."

The other agreed. "We didn't get a long look, but it wasn't a bear."

Jacobi looked back at Ash. "You said you know a thing or two about cryptids?"

Ash nodded. "Yeah. I host a cryptid podcast pretty much for fun. Sasquatch, dogman, aliens, paranormal stuff, really. I always wanted to see one. Thought I'd be excited. Proof, right? But standing there, watching it crawl across that roof... I just wanted to disappear. I didn't want to believe my eyes."

Beretti's tone stayed calm. "Any chance it was a person? Someone pulling a prank?"

Ash shook his head. "No. No. You don't fake something like that. That wasn't a person in a costume. You could feel it. It didn't belong here, and it didn't move like anything I have ever seen before."

Jacobi stepped forward, offering a handshake. "Thanks

for talking to us."

Beretti looked at the other two. "And you're both okay?"

"Yeah," they both said flatly.

"If anything else comes to mind," she said, "call the sheriff's office. Even if it feels small."

Ash hesitated. "Do you believe me?"

Beretti met his eyes. "We believe something happened. And what you saw fits with reports we've had in the past."

Ash let out a shaky breath. "Alright. That helps. A little."

They turned to leave. As they started walking back toward the loop, Ash called out, "Hey... you're not like those Men in Black types, right? Gonna wipe my memory or haul me off somewhere?"

Jacobi looked over his shoulder. "No."

They kept walking. Behind them, Ash and his friends went quiet.

As the agents passed between tents and back to the sheriff, Jacobi glanced toward the woods.

"That kid's not sleeping tonight."

"Nope. Another case of "be careful what you wish for," Beretti replied.

CHAPTER 5

The afternoon sun had started its slow drift behind the western ridge as Beretti and Jacobi stepped away from the campsite loop. They spotted Sheriff Beretti leaning against the hood of his cruiser, arms crossed, his radio clipped but quiet.

He glanced up as they approached, squinting slightly in the light. "How'd it go with the McMillan kid?"

Beretti stopped beside him. "I believe him. Saw it real clear too."

Jacobi added, "Seems to be convinced he saw a Dogman. Follows cryptid stuff online."

Ben gave a half-smile. "Well, he ain't the only one." Pushing off the cruiser and nodding toward the lot. "Come on. Let's grab some food. I'll fill you in."

They followed him into town, a ten-minute drive from the campground. The roads twisted through clusters of tall redwoods and open farmland, the town of Blackridge resting low in the valley like it had settled in for good and didn't plan on leaving.

Lunch was at an old diner off Mayford Street. A faded sign reading *Millie's* swung gently in the breeze, the edges sun-bleached and curling. Inside, the place smelled like frying onions, fresh coffee and pine cleaner. The booths were worn but clean, the waitress behind the counter already filling water glasses as they took a seat near the back.

Ben ordered a cheeseburger and fries. Jacobi got the same. Beretti asked for a turkey club, no mayo.

When the waitress disappeared, Ben sat back with a sigh and stretched. "So. You wanna know about the history, or just the recent mess?"

Beretti looked at him. "Start where it makes sense. For Jacobi."

Ben folded his hands on the table. "Alright. Long story short, the people around here have known about the Sasquatch for decades. Maybe longer. My grandfather used to talk about them like they were bears or mountain lions. Just part of the woods."

Jacobi tilted his head slightly. "You're saying the whole town knows?"

"Not everyone," Ben replied. "New folks move in, tourists pass through, they don't know nothing. But the ones who've been here a while? The farmers, the hunters, the folks up in the hills? Yeah. They know."

Jacobi leaned forward slightly. "And they're okay with it?"

Ben tilted his head slightly. "Most are. Sasquatch don't bother people much. Keep to the deeper woods. Every once in a while someone has a run-in. A sighting. Hell, we had a guy ten years ago who swore one saved his kid from a bear. Others say they've been followed or had rocks thrown at them. Depends on who you ask."

Jacobi gave a low whistle. "Sounds like coexistence."

"Pretty much," Ben said. "At least until a week ago."

Their food arrived, plates hitting the table with a soft clink. No one touched anything right away.

Ben continued, "First call I got was from a farmer. Lives out past Pine Road. Said one of his cows died overnight. Old thing, already sick. But when he went out to move the body, he saw something crouched next to it."

Beretti tilted her head. "What kind of something?"

"His words? A goddamn nightmare. Said it looked like a wolf, but massive. Hunched over the carcass like it was guarding it. Not eating like a scavenger. When it saw him, it stood up. On two legs. Watched him. Then walked off."

Jacobi finally picked up a fry. "Walked?"

"Walked," Ben confirmed. "Not ran. No fear. Just turned and left."

Beretti's voice was calm. "This farmer willing to talk?"

"Yeah. Name's Clay Darrow. Been on that land for forty years. Never seen anything like it. You can head over after we eat."

Jacobi tapped the side of his glass. "You think that was the first?"

"The first we heard about, yeah. Next one came maybe a day later. Teenagers were having a party behind one of their parents' houses, near the forest east of town."

"Bonfire, music, typical weekend stuff."

Beretti didn't look away. "What happened?"

Ben's expression hardened. "Two kids got attacked. One of them, girl named Rina Havel, lost her leg. The other, Tyler Cruz, got torn up across the chest and back. Doctors say he'll pull through, but he's gonna have scars for life."

Jacobi's voice dropped. "Where were the others?"

"Most of them ran, fast," Ben said. "A few caught a glimpse and swore they saw a wolf in the trees. Not on the ground, but up in the branches. Then it jumped and hit hard. After that, things got out of control."

Beretti blinked. "A wolf in the trees?"

"Yup. Just watching them," Ben replied as he took a sip of his drink.

Jacobi looked intrigued. "No wolves in this region, right?"

"Closest confirmed pack's almost two hundred miles north," Ben said. "We've got coyotes, the odd big cat, but no wolves. Never have. You get the odd drifter from up north but nothing like this."

Beretti shifted slowly. "And since then?"

"Livestock disappearances. Someone's goat pen got

ripped clean open. It's not just the number of reports, it's the pattern. These things are getting braver."

Jacobi leaned back. "You said 'these things.' You think there's more than one?"

Ben didn't answer right away. He picked up his burger, took a bite, then set it down and wiped his mouth.

"I don't know. Might be one. Might be more. But more than four reports in just over a week? That's too much for a single animal, even one with a big range."

Beretti asked quietly, "What about the Sasquatch?"

Ben looked up at her. "They're not gonna like this. Whatever this is, it's not from here. And I've got a feeling the old guard in those woods is watching. Waiting to see if this thing crosses a line."

Jacobi met his eyes. "And if it does?"

Ben shrugged. "Then we might not be dealing with a creature problem. We might be looking at a war."

Silence settled between them while the steady drone of the diner carried on around them. The quiet clink of cutlery, the whir of a milkshake machine, and a distant laugh from the kitchen filled the space. Their booth, though, remained untouched by it all as they ate their lunch.

Beretti finally broke the silence. "Alright. Let's talk to Clay."

They finished eating quickly, paid the bill, and stepped outside into the shifting light. The wind had picked up a little as townsfolk went about their business.

Ben pointed down the road, glancing at Jacobi. "Nicole knows where Pine Road is. Take the main strip to Maple, hang a right. It's just past the edge of town. You'll see a big rust-red barn on the left. That's Clay's place. He's grumpy but honest."

"Sounds like me every morning," Jacobi quipped.

Ben opened his cruiser door but paused. "Keep me posted. And be careful. This thing might be moving during the day now...."

Beretti replied. "We will."

Ben offered a small wave. "See you at home."

The two agents got into their vehicle and pulled away, heading down the quiet road out of town. Ahead, the hills sloped gently into pine-lined farmland. In the distance, a dilapidated tractor sat like a sentinel among the trees.

Jacobi adjusted his seat and glanced out the window. "What do you think happens if the Sasquatch catch wind of the Dogman?"

Beretti kept her eyes on the road. "They'd already know. They're watching. Probably trying to figure out if it's going to move on."

"And if it doesn't?"

She exhaled, slow and even. "Then it becomes a bigger problem. Not much anyone can do when those two worlds collide."

Neither of them spoke after that.

CHAPTER 6

THE DOGMAN

The forest was old. Too old. It reeked of moss, rot and things that had ruled before time had names. But beneath that rot was power. And he could smell it.

The land here belonged to the others. The tall ones. The quiet ones. They walked like ghosts and moved like wind. But they had grown soft. Hidden too long in caves and silence, worshipping balance while the world burned around them.

He remembered a time before that. When fear walked on two legs and hunted in packs. His kind had roamed freely then, claiming what they needed, tearing through weakness, obeying only instinct and hunger. But the tall ones had forced them back. Beaten them. Taken what should have been theirs.

No more.

The land he had come from was dying. Trees brittle and dry. Prey harder to find. The hairless ones had pushed in closer with their machines and fire, cutting away at what little was left. His kind had begun turning on each other, fighting for scraps, forgetting what they once were. The old paths were lost, the howls unanswered. He refused to starve alongside the desperate and the broken. He had left before it could take him too.

He had tested their borders, watched their patterns, scented their trails, marked the edges with blood. The tall ones didn't fight like they used to. They protected, yes. But they feared too. That fear had a smell. And he liked it.

The territory wasn't just ground and trees. It was shelter. Food. Safe breeding. Dominance.

It was legacy.

If he took this land, others would come. The howl would return to the high ridges, and no one, tall or small, would stop it.

He stalked to the edge of a clearing, crouching low, golden eyes narrowing on a place where moss still held their scent. He had watched them, waited, biding his time. Sooner or later, there would be a sick one. A lonesome one. And then he would strike.

One by one. Until the land was his.

This land would be his.

CHAPTER 7

The road narrowed as they drove deeper in, curling between rows of pine and sagging old fences. Jacobi cracked his window when they turned onto Pine Road, letting in the dry scent of bark and sun-warmed earth. The light shifted lower, flickering through the trees in broken bands. Up ahead, a red barn came into view, its paint dulled by time but the frame holding steady.

Beretti slowed as the tires bumped into the dirt drive. A rusted mailbox hung crookedly near the fence, "Darrow" hand-painted across it in flaking black letters. The house sat back from the road, modest but well-kept, with a wraparound porch and an old wind chime gently stirring in the breeze.

A man was sitting on a wooden bench near the barn, cleaning what looked to be a lever-action rifle. He glanced up as they pulled in, then stood slowly, wiping his hands on a rag.

Beretti parked and stepped out first.

"Clay Darrow?" she called.

The man squinted at her, then nodded. "That's me."

Jacobi came around the other side of the SUV, badge in hand but kept low and informal. "We're with the FBI. Special Agents Beretti and Jacobi. We appreciate you taking the time."

The man's eyes lingered on Beretti. "Beretti, huh?"

She gave a polite smile. "Sheriff Ben Beretti is my uncle."

Clay blinked, then chuckled. "Well, I'll be damned. You're the girl who used to come with him out to the 4-H shows. You were what, eleven, twelve? Always had your hair wild and never wore shoes."

Beretti laughed under her breath. "That was me."

"Guess time sneaks up on us all," Clay said, motioning toward the porch. "Come on up. Might as well sit if we're talkin' about monsters."

They followed him to the porch. Jacobi sat on the railing, with his back to the field. Beretti took the chair nearest the door, notebook in hand but not open yet. Clay leaned against the post, the rifle resting by his boot.

"You mind walking us through what happened?" Jacobi asked. "Sheriff Beretti mentioned you had a run-in of some kind."

"Yeah. Damn right I did, kid." Clay rubbed the side of his neck, eyes drifting toward the pasture. "Let's see… would've been about a week or so ago now, I guess. Definitely somethin' I'll never forget."

"Started with one of my old cows dyin' sometime just after dark. I noticed it but figured I'd deal with it in the morning. She was already sick. Winter's hard on the older ones."

"What time did you head out?" Beretti asked.

"Bit after five. Still early, sun barely up. I do my walk every morning, check the fence line, carry the rifle. Habit."

He leaned forward slightly, voice a little lower.

"From a ways off, I see something movin' on the carcass. Figure it's a coyote or two, maybe a bear. Happens sometimes. I start walking in slow, like I always do. Nothin' rushed. Wasn't worried."

Jacobi's tone stayed relaxed. "How close did you get?"

"Maybe ninety yards, give or take. Then I stopped and pulled up the rifle to get a better look through the scope. I always check first before firin'."

"And what did you see?" Jacobi asked.

Clay paused, his eyes fixed on the field again. The memory lingered there, tucked somewhere he didn't like to go.

"At first, just this shape. Big. Real big. I could see the back of it, shoulders hunched, kind of rockin' like it was chewing or pullin' at my old cow. Dark fur. Not black, more like... charcoal. Dirty-lookin'. Mangy in spots."

"I kept watchin', trying to figure out what I was lookin' at. I ain't seen nuthin' like it before. It had a tail, I think, but real short. Legs were bent strange. Knees pointed the wrong way. And the head... that's what got me."

He drew in a breath and finally looked at them.

"Wolf. Straight up. Snout, ears, thick neck. Only it was huge. Not just big like a German Shepherd or a Malamute, I mean heavy. Broad. It didn't move like a four-legger either. Sorta hunched, yeah, but upright. Like it was comfortable ya know?"

Jacobi exchanged a glance with Beretti. "Did it see you?"

"Oh yeah," Clay said, almost with a shiver. "It stopped eatin', lifted its head real slow, and turned right toward me like it knew I was watchin'. I could see what was hangin' from its mouth."

Beretti spoke softly. "Entrails?"

Clay gave a slow nod. "Pink and red. Stringy. Drippin' like spaghetti from its jaw. It just stared at me with these yellow eyes, and then it snarled. Showed every damn tooth. I nearly fell on my ass."

He chuckled once, but it didn't carry humor. "That was no damn wolf. That was somethin' evil."

"What happened next?" Jacobi asked.

"The freakin' thing stood up, if you can believe that. Straight. On two damn legs. Just like a man. Broad chest. Long arms. Fingers. I swear it had hands. Clawed, but real fingers. It watched me for a second, then just... turned and walked off toward the tree line like it had all the time in the world. Wasn't afraid of me one bit."

Beretti narrowed her eyes. "Did it run at any point?"

"Nope. Acted like it owned the place," Clay said as he shook his head.

Jacobi asked, "What did you do?"

Clay rubbed his chin. "Nothin'. I was too frozen to move. After a bit, I backed up slow all the way to the house. Didn't even put the rifle down till I locked the door. Sat inside for hours just thinkin'. Figured no one would believe me, but then I heard about what happened to those kids."

Beretti flipped her notebook open and jotted a few notes. "Have you ever seen anything like that before? Even close?"

Clay's voice turned dry. "Hell no. Bigfoot now, sure. Once or twice. Never up close, but you catch a shape, hear the howls and the crackin' of branches off trail. Loud bastards. I figure most of them don't want trouble. But this thing? This thing wasn't shy. It didn't care two hoots that I saw it."

Jacobi asked, "Would you say this creature was similar to a Sasquatch?"

"Not even close," Clay said without hesitation. "Sasquatch is big and bulky, sure, but this... this had a meanness to it. It was built like a lean bodybuilder. All muscle, no fat, and a massive back. You could see every part of it flex when it moved."

Beretti nodded slowly. "We appreciate you talking to us, Clay. It helps to have a clear picture."

"Yeah, well, I ain't sleepin' much anyway these days. I still walk my fence in the morning, but I don't go past the barn. Not till full light. That field don't feel right anymore."

Jacobi stood up straight. "If you think of anything else, even small details, give us a call. Here's my number."

He handed Clay a card, which the older man accepted without much ceremony.

Beretti shook his hand. "Good seeing you again."

Clay gave her a small smile. "Didn't think I'd be talkin' monsters with the Beretti girl, but here we are."

They left him standing on the porch, wind stirring the hem of his jacket as he watched them go.

Back in the SUV, Jacobi buckled his seatbelt but didn't say anything for a few seconds.

Beretti started the engine and glanced at him. "What?"

"That guy's been around. He knows what a bear or coyote looks like."

"He wasn't making it up." Beretti replied as she started the SUV.

"Not even a little," Jacobi said.

The sun was slipping lower as they pulled out of the drive and turned back toward the road. Fields rolled past in silence.

The forest ahead looked darker than it had an hour ago.

CHAPTER 8

THE SCOUT

He moved like the wind between trees. No sound. No pause. Just breath, and instinct, and memory.

The moss beneath his feet was soft and damp, spongy from the night rain. Above, a red sun filtered through a patchwork of old-growth pine and spruce. Ravens circled high and distant, silent today. That unsettled him.

Dakkar was known as the watcher among his kind. The one who moved along the perimeter of their lands while the others rested. He had no need for words. Not the kind the hairless ones used. His people spoke through scent and gesture, through the quiet of movement and the shift of weight in the soil. There was no deception in that. No noise. Only truth.

His frame was broad and thick with muscle layered under coarse, dark hair. His arms hung longer than his knees, his gait built for both upright movement and rapid descent through forested slopes. He could run just as well and fast on four limbs when needed, his body shifting effortlessly between postures. His feet, wide and calloused, sank quietly into the forest floor. Light barely touched the contours of his face beneath the shadow of his sloping brow and heavy mane. Where others might be seen, Dakkar vanished.

He had been born in the high caves above the lake, beneath a thunderstorm that cracked stone and drove elk to stampede. The elder had once called him strong-of-step. His first memory was of standing on a wet stone ledge, watching cloud shadows sweep across the water. His mother was long gone now. His father had disappeared into the mountain one winter and never returned.

This land was in his blood. It pulsed beneath his calloused hands and hardened soles. The trees remembered him. The roots whispered when he passed. And now, something was changing.

He crouched at the edge of a ridge where deer came to drink. A stream ran below, glistening in slivers of sun. But the water smelled wrong. Not just iron. There was a sourness beneath it, like blood turned stale and something fouler beneath that. Oily. Diseased. The scent didn't belong to anything that lived clean.

His head lifted. Eyes narrowed.

Kreth.

Sharp teeth on two legs.

He had not seen them in many cycles. Long ago, before the trees grew thick and the hairless ones forgot how to listen, the Kreth had passed through in cold months. Searching. Always hungry. But never brave enough to stay. There had been an unspoken law between the kinds. A law older than fire.

You do not linger where the roots remember. Not in these woods.

Now that law was breaking.

He stood and followed the scent, moving like mist through the trees. It was fresher than he wanted. Days old. Carried on wind. Settled into bark. Sweat. Meat. Blood. And something oily that clung to the nostrils. Kreth stench.

Not just one.

He stopped at the remains of a rabbit, torn through the

middle and flung in two pieces across the roots of a fallen cedar. The kill was wasteful. The Kreth had not eaten it. Just shredded it. Left its blood to pool and draw stink-wings.

He touched the bark nearby. Deep gouges. Spread wide. Fresh.

They were testing. Pushing.

He pressed his knuckles into the dirt and closed his eyes. A slow exhale through flared nostrils. The other scouts had said nothing, but he had seen them glance toward the hills more often lately. Even the old ones had grown restless, staring at the horizon for longer than they should. One of the juveniles had come back with a deep scratch down his shoulder and refused to say how it happened.

He rose and moved again, deeper into the boundary trails. This was the edge of their domain, marked in ancient ways. Stones stacked in silent piles. Claw marks hidden behind moss. Sap rubbed from trees where the scent lingered strong. Limbs woven high among the branches, bent and twisted to speak without sound. Only his kind would recognize them. And only the Kreth would dare to challenge them.

They had no such respect for old things.

By dusk, the clouds had gathered low and thick. He

crouched beneath a leaning birch and waited.

The wind shifted.

They were close.

He did not see them yet, but he felt them. The air had turned sour, thick with the scent of damp fur and old blood. The usual rhythms were gone. The squirrels did not chatter. The foxes stayed in their dens. Even the birds, high in the canopy, held still. Not out of respect. Out of fear.

He crouched lower. Eyes steady. Breath held.

Then movement.

To the left, through a curtain of fern and alder, he saw the flicker of muscle and fur. Gray-brown. Long limbs. It moved with purpose, not fear. And behind it, a second. Larger. Broader. Both hunched low. Sniffing. Watching. Weaving through the forest like predators who believed they belonged.

He waited.

The larger one stopped near the boundary marker. It sniffed the moss-covered stones. Then growled. The sound was low and guttural, vibrating through the earth like a challenge. It kicked the marker pile apart with a careless swing of its clawed hand.

A line had been crossed.

He rose from his crouch, standing to full height, shoulders broad and still.

The Kreth froze.

The forest seemed to pause, caught between one breath and the next.

The larger Kreth crouched low, breath fogging in the chilled air. Muscles rippled under tangled, coarse hair, its long arms ending in black, curled claws. The smaller one stayed back, shifting side to side, eyes glinting yellow behind tangled bristles.

Dakkar stepped forward once, a silent warning.

Then the larger Kreth bared its teeth.

It leapt.

Dakkar didn't wait. He twisted to the side and dropped low, letting the claws slash past his shoulder. As it turned, Dakkar drove his shoulder into its ribs. Bone met bone. The Kreth staggered, but didn't fall.

Behind him, the smaller one charged.

He pivoted. His massive arm swept sideways and caught the second creature in the chest. It lifted off its feet and crashed into a tree trunk, bark splintering under the impact. The larger one was already circling back, fast and low, claws dragging through the dirt.

Dakkar drew upright and let it come.

At the last second, he surged forward and locked its arms, pushing it backward in a shuddering clash of limbs. They slammed into a thicket of young saplings, snapping branches. The Kreth snarled inches from his face, spittle flying. It clawed at his side, raking hair and skin, but Dakkar held his grip. He drove a knee into the beast's midsection. Once. Twice. A third time. It howled and buckled, and he flung it sideways into the brush.

The smaller one had recovered.

It leapt from the shadows, jaws wide, teeth flashing.

Dakkar dropped to all fours.

His motion was sudden and seamless, weight transferring with fluid control. He burst forward under the pounce and turned, catching the beast mid-air. His claws dug deep into its back as he rolled, using the creature's own momentum to slam it down hard. A crack echoed through the trees.

He rose fast.

The smaller Kreth twitched, legs curling, but didn't rise.

The larger one came again.

This time it didn't leap. It crept forward slowly, claws spread, eyes locked. Blood ran down one side of its face where a branch had scored its cheek.

Dakkar squared himself.

The scent of the dying Kreth lingered, thick in the air. The stream nearby trickled faintly, steady and indifferent. Every nerve in his body was aware. Every breath belonged to the moment.

The two circled each other, slow steps crunching twigs and frost. Dakkar watched the rhythm of the creature's body, its weight shifting left, then right. Then left again. He knew what came next.

It struck.

He deflected the first claw, letting it rake past his forearm. The second he caught. Their arms locked, claws digging into flesh. The Kreth bit toward his throat, but Dakkar twisted, pulling them both off-balance. They hit the ground in a tangle of limbs, rolling hard down a shallow incline. Dirt flew. Stones rolled. Blood soaked into the forest floor.

At the bottom, Dakkar was first to rise.

He gripped the Kreth's arm and yanked it forward. His forehead smashed into the creature's snout. Bone crunched. The Kreth shrieked, staggering backward with blood spraying from its broken nose.

Dakkar did not stop.

He struck again. His fists slammed against the creature's chest It fell to its knees. He circled behind, gripped its head in both hands, and twisted. A single, brutal snap.

The Kreth fell.

He stood over the body, chest heaving, arms coated in blood both dark and bright. His left shoulder burned, gouged by claws. A cut along his thigh ran warm, but not deep.

He turned and looked toward the trees.

No others followed.

Still, he waited.

He listened.

Nothing but the slow return of forest sound. Distant birds. A shift in the canopy above. The wind moving again.

He stepped back toward the boundary marker. The stones lay scattered across the path, their scent diluted by Kreth filth.

He paused near the bodies.

One at a time, he lifted them. The weight was manageable. Dead muscle hung loose. He carried them both, one over each shoulder, and began walking.

He moved through the forest for a long stretch, putting distance between the kill site and where the others might travel. When the wind changed and the trees began to thin, he slowed.

The place stank before he saw it.

It was not part of the forest. The trees stopped growing here, as if refusing to spread their roots. The air turned foul, clinging to his throat and hair. Even the stink-wings changed.

They didn't flee.

They gathered.

They swarmed over the broken mounds, buzzing thick around his head, drawn to the rot like it sang to them.

Ahead, the land sank into a wide pit of broken things. Rotting piles of cast-off refuse from the hairless ones, reeking of decay and something sweet and sour that turned the stomach. Shattered shapes jutted from the ground. Ripped things, bent things, hollow things with no scent of life. A place that repelled the senses.

He had come upon it once as a young scout and never returned. No animal made a den here. Nothing healed here.

He knew the hairless ones brought their dead things to this place.

Now, so would he.

He moved down the slope, his breathing shallow. The stench was overwhelming, thick enough to taste. Even the wind seemed poisoned.

As he approached the mound of filth, he dropped the Kreth.

Their bodies landed in a heap, partly on the dirt, partly on the mound of crumbling waste. Stink-wings stirred. Sky-pickers circled but did not cry out.

Dakkar stared at them for a moment, his expression unreadable.

He turned away.

Back through the trees. Through clean air. Through living things.

He returned to the marker.

He crouched and began to rebuild the pile. Each stone placed carefully, deliberately. When it was done, he pressed his hand to the largest one and let his scent sink in.

Not just a warning.

A claim.

He would return with the signs. The blood. The scents. The broken law.

The others would need to know. This was not a stray. Not a lost beast wandering from burnt lands.

This was the start of something larger.

The Kreth were coming.

And Dakkar, scout of the old kind, would be ready.

CHAPTER 9

The road into town was quieter now, the sun sinking behind the ridge and casting the streets in soft winter gold. Beretti took the turns from instinct, her hands loose on the wheel, guiding the SUV past familiar corners and storefronts that hadn't changed much since she was a teenager.

There were quite a few motorbikes scattered along the curbs and parking lots. Jacobi glanced out the window.

"Lot of bikes in town."

Beretti looked out the window. "Oh yeah. They're here for the *Ironhowl Run.*"

They passed the corner gas station, the feed store and the old community hall before slowing in front of a small grocery with a flickering neon "OPEN" sign in the window. Beretti pulled into the angled spot out front.

"Two minutes," she said, unbuckling. "I want to bring a bottle to dinner."

Jacobi followed her inside. The place was quiet, a couple of locals browsing the aisles. The floor squeaked underfoot as they made their way to the back where the wine was stacked. Beretti grabbed a bottle of local red, then turned to see Jacobi a few steps away, eyeing a wire bucket filled with wrapped bouquets.

He picked one up, thoughtful. "For Leoni?"

Beretti smiled. "She's going to be putting up with you for a few days. Flowers are a good start."

They checked out quickly. The cashier, a young guy with sleepy eyes and a ball cap, rang them up with barely a word.

Beretti scanned her work-issued VISA.

"I've got it," she said, not looking up.

Jacobi didn't argue. He just followed her back out into the cooling evening.

"You're not half bad at this small-town diplomacy thing," Beretti said as Jacobi slid the flowers into the back seat.

"I'm just trying not to get us kicked out before dinner."

They pulled into the driveway of a low, single-story home with deep eaves and olive-green siding. A string of solar lights lit the porch rail, flickering gently as the sun disappeared behind the ridge. Beretti cut the engine and sat for a moment.

"He's not home yet," she said, scanning the driveway. "His truck's not here."

Jacobi unbuckled. "Should we come back?"

"No," she said, already opening her door. "Leoni will be here."

They walked up the steps and before Beretti could knock, the front door opened.

Leoni stood in the doorway, hands on her hips, a wide smile forming beneath bright blue eyes and a mop of silver-streaked curly hair. She wore a brightly patterned cardigan over a sunflower-yellow tee and soft, well-worn jeans. Her eyes lit up when she saw Beretti.

"Well look what the wind dragged in," Leoni said, stepping forward to pull her into a hug.

Beretti hugged her back with real warmth. "Hi, Leoni. Sorry for the short notice."

"You're never a bother," Leoni said, waving her off. She turned toward Jacobi with a curious look. "And you must be Noah."

"Guilty," he said with a grin, reaching out for a handshake. In his other hand, he held out a small bouquet of fresh flowers.

"For you," he added.

Leoni's eyes lit up. She took them gently and smiled. "Thank you. What a nice surprise. These are my favorite."

Without missing a beat, she pulled him into a big, unapologetic hug. "Come on in. I've got a kettle going, and the casserole's in the oven. Figured you two would be hungry."

She stepped back to let them through, giving Jacobi a once-over with a grin before glancing at Beretti. "Yep. I can see why you chose him as a partner."

Beretti didn't reply, just gave her a look that said behave.

They stepped inside. The house smelled like beef and rosemary, warm and savory, with hints of roasted vegetables lingering underneath. Same as always. The warmth in the entry hit her like a blanket, soft lighting and creaky floorboards wrapping around them.

Almost immediately, two dogs trotted into the hallway. A spry little Jack Russell cross darted toward Beretti, tail wagging so fast it blurred.

"Hey, Whiskey," Beretti said, crouching to rub behind the dog's ears. The Jack Russell was already halfway onto her back, legs twitching in expectation, clearly anticipating the belly rub.

The second dog followed at a slower, grumpier pace. A shaggy Silky cross with one eye and a slightly crooked gait ambled toward Jacobi, sniffed his boot, and gave a soft grunt before wandering off.

Jacobi watched him go. "Friend or foe?"

Leoni smiled as she shut the door. "That's Wink. Don't let the stink-eye fool you. He's a marshmallow. Just don't move his blanket or you'll get the side-eye of doom."

"They're spoiled," Beretti added, standing again. "Basically the kids around here."

Whiskey jumped onto the couch and circled once before flopping down. Wink hoisted himself up beside her and leaned in, one eye still fixed on the guests like he was keeping a ledger.

Jacobi glanced around the living room. "You've got a nice place."

"Ben built most of it himself," Beretti said, slipping off her coat. "Before Leoni moved in, it was just wood, tools and caffeine."

Leoni looked up from the kitchen. "And then I civilized it. Mostly."

Jacobi kicked his boots off at the door and followed Beretti into the living room. She dropped onto the couch like someone who knew exactly how it would feel. Jacobi settled into the armchair and scanned the nearby bookshelf stacked with crime novels, cookbooks, and old framed photos.

One caught his eye. "Is that him with Tom Selleck?"

Beretti nodded. "The look-alike contest."

Leoni came in with a tray of mugs and a plate of shortbread cookies. "Still proud of that. I sent in the photo without telling him."

She set everything down and stood up straight. "Ben's wrapping something up at the station. He'll be home any minute. You've got time to warm up."

"Thanks, Leoni," Beretti said, wrapping her hands around a mug. "This is perfect."

Jacobi leaned back and let out a sigh, stretching his legs out. "This is dangerously cozy. You might not get me back in the SUV."

Leoni passed him the cookie plate with a wink. "Good. You look like you could use a little spoiling."

Beretti gave them both a look, amused but already bracing for the teasing to come.

The conversation drifted from small-town updates to stories from the field. Jacobi shared a story about a case in Michigan involving footprints and a very territorial raccoon. Even Whiskey gave a sneeze that might've been laughter.

Then Jacobi's phone buzzed on the coffee table.

He leaned forward and checked the screen. "Unknown number. Local area code," he said, frowning slightly.

Beretti watched him pick it up. "This is Agent Jacobi."

"Hey, it's Clay Darrow. Sorry to call out of the blue... Jolene just looked at me and said, 'You didn't tell them about the howls, did you?' I told her no, and she called me a damn fool and told me to fix it."

Jacobi smiled faintly and tapped the speaker button.

"Smart woman. You've got our attention, Clay."

"Figured you'd want to know. Past few nights I've been hearin' more of them."

"The Sasquatch?" Jacobi asked.

"Pretty sure. I hear 'em now and then. A howl here, a knock there. Nothing to write home about. But lately, it's been... more. Last three nights, it's been constant. Long howls, different directions, even a couple of returns. Almost like they're calling to each other. Or warning."

Beretti leaned in, her expression sharpening. "You ever heard it like that before?"

"Not in many years," Clay said. "And not this clear. They're movin' around more too. I don't know if it's because of that thing I saw or if somethin' else is pokin' the nest."

"Hard to say," Jacobi said quietly.

Beretti asked, "What does your gut say, Clay?"

Clay paused. "My gut says they're restless. And when they're restless, I keep the lights on and my rifle close."

"Thanks for calling," Jacobi said. "Tell Jolene she's got good instincts. We appreciate the heads-up."

Clay gave a dry chuckle. "She'd agree with you. Take care, Agents."

The call ended, and Jacobi set the phone back down on the table.

Leoni, quiet through the exchange, glanced between them. "That didn't sound good."

"No, it didn't," Jacobi said. "If they're making this much noise, it means something's off."

Beretti leaned back, eyes drifting to the window as the street lights flickered.

"They're watching. Listening. Figuring out how far they'll let it go."

No one said anything for a while.

The dogs dozed on the couch. The wind bumped against the window. From the kitchen, the oven ticked softly as it cooled.

Somewhere beyond the edges of town, the woods stood ancient and patient.

A war was already being waged beneath their canopy.

CHAPTER 10

The front door opened just as Jacobi was placing the last fork on the table. Cold air swept in with Ben, his boots thudding against the hardwood as he stepped inside, shoulders squared beneath his sheriff's jacket.

"Smells good in here," Ben said, brushing a leaf off his sleeve. "I'm not too late, am I?"

"Perfect timing," Beretti called from the kitchen. "Table's just about set."

Leoni stood near the oven, tugging a steaming casserole from the rack with a proud little grin. "Dinner waits for no one in this house, Sheriff, but I made an exception."

Ben chuckled and shrugged out of his coat, hanging it on the wall hook. "Appreciate it."

Jacobi stepped back to give him room. "You missed the

hard part. I had to fold napkins."

Leoni raised an eyebrow. "He crushed it, though. Might have a future in dinner parties."

Beretti smirked. "Don't encourage him."

Ben glanced around the kitchen, the warmth of the oven and low lighting softening the edges of the long day. "Hope you didn't go to any trouble."

"I always go to trouble," Leoni said, setting the bubbling dish in the center of the table. "That's how you know it's made with love. Or irritation. Hard to tell the difference."

As they sat down, Beretti reached for the wine bottle she had brought earlier. "Thought this might go well with dinner."

"Ooh," Leoni said, grabbing glasses. "Fancy agent wine. Anyone want a glass?"

Jacobi raised a hand. "Sure. Just one."

Ben waved it off. "Not for me."

Beretti shook her head. "I'm good."

Leoni poured one glass and handed it to Jacobi, then filled

the others with water. "Alright. Dig in before it goes cold."

The casserole had a golden, bubbling top, rich with roasted garlic and melted cheese. Steam curled from the green beans next to it, and a basket of warm rolls sat nearby. The meal had the kind of comfort only home cooking could offer.

Conversation stayed light at first. Jacobi asked how long Leoni had been putting up with Ben. She answered with a cheeky grin and a story about him getting stuck under the house trying to fix a pipe and refusing to call a plumber out of pride.

Ben grunted. "You tell one embarrassing story, and it sticks with you forever."

Jacobi laughed. "In fairness, it's a pretty good one."

They passed dishes around, plates refilled more than once. The warmth of the food and the ease of the company smoothed out the edge of the day.

After dinner, Leoni stood to gather the plates.

"I'll help," Beretti said, stacking a few.

"You sit," Leoni replied. "You're technically a guest.

Besides, I'm territorial in the kitchen."

Beretti held her hands up in mock surrender.

They sat for another half hour, the low murmur of the local news playing on the TV while no one really watched.

Ben stood and stretched, rubbing his neck. "You two should get some sleep."

Jacobi looked down the hall. "Which one is me?"

Beretti stepped around the table. "I've got you. This way."

He followed her past the living room, the low hum of the heater rising as the house settled in for the night. She opened the door to the room at the end of the hall.

"Extra blankets in the chest if you need them," she said. "And keep the door shut unless you want Whiskey trying to share your pillow."

Jacobi stepped inside, setting his bag down. "Might not be a bad thing."

Beretti lingered a moment. "Sleep well. Tomorrow, we hit the ground running."

He offered a faint smile. "Looking forward to it."

Turning, she walked back down the hallway, enveloped in the warmth of her home and family. It wasn't exactly peace, but it was something close, and in this line of work, that was more than enough.

CHAPTER 11

Barbara rinsed the last of the dinner dishes and set the damp towel over the oven handle. The clock on the microwave blinked 9:47. Joel had already gone to bed an hour ago, like clockwork, same as every night. He never said much after dinner. Just shuffled off with his bad knees and mumbled something about the early weather report.

She didn't mind. Joel wasn't the talkative type, and after twenty-eight years in the same modest home just outside of town, they'd found a rhythm that worked. He'd turn in early. She'd tidy up, double-check the doors, and finish the day with her quiet ritual, a smoke, and a single shot of whiskey out on the screened porch. Just one. It helped her sleep.

The back porch wrapped around the side of the house, screened in with old mesh and aluminium trim they'd replaced twice in the last decade. The boards creaked a little when she stepped out, but it was a familiar sound. A part of the house she trusted.

Barbara settled onto the old wicker sofa with its faded cushions and lit her cigarette. The glow of the cherry was soft in the dark. She sipped her whiskey, smooth and biting. Around her, the trees whispered in the distance. The land sloped down beyond their yard into a thin stretch of woods. Past that, fields and silence. The stars shimmered above the black outline of the ridge, and the porch light cast a dull yellow cone across the steps.

She breathed in the cool air. The house felt so much bigger now that the kids had all moved out, married, scattered. There were toys in other living rooms now. Pictures on other refrigerators. That was okay. Barbara had made her peace with it.

Tonight was colder than it had been all week. She pulled her cardigan tighter and listened to the chirping of night frogs, the dry clicking of crickets. A barred owl hooted once from deeper in the trees, long and low.

And then, all at once, everything stopped.

The silence didn't come gradually. It was as if the volume had been cut. One second, the night was alive. The next, it was hollow.

Barbara held her cigarette mid-air. She frowned and turned her head slowly, listening. Nothing. No rustling. No insects. Even the trees had gone still.

She looked out across the yard. Her eyes took a second to adjust. At first, she thought maybe it was a passing cloud overhead, but the stars were still there, clear and cold. The stillness wasn't above. It was all around.

She exhaled deeply, heart thumping in a way she hadn't felt in years. Unease settled in her chest like an extra weight.

Probably a fox. Or a coyote somewhere near. That would shut the others up.

Still, she couldn't shake the feeling of dread. Her cigarette burned low. She took another sip of whiskey, forcing her shoulders to relax. "Don't be ridiculous," she mumbled, and brought the cigarette back to her lips.

A pair of reddish-amber lights hovered at the edge of the trees, about sixty yards away. Low to the ground. She squinted, leaning forward a little.

Deer, maybe. But no, deer had eyes on the sides of their heads, and these were forward-facing. Flat. Focused. Like something watching. And there was no reflection from her porch light. They seemed to glow on their own.

She narrowed her eyes. The lights didn't move. Just hung there, motionless, about a foot off the ground.

They blinked.

Barbara froze. Her hand trembled slightly, whiskey sloshing in the glass. The cigarette burned down to her fingers before she noticed and cursed softly, stubbing it out in the old ashtray beside her. When she looked back up, her breath caught.

Three more pairs of eyes had appeared, flickering into existence two at a time, each as still and unnatural as the first.

She gripped the edge of the cushion, mouth dry. "Joel," she whispered, though she didn't move. Her legs felt rooted, but her instincts screamed to get inside.

The first set of eyes began to rise.

Not forward. Not closer. Up.

As they climbed, the air filled with a sickening crunch, wet and heavy, like bones being snapped into place. A sharp jolt of nausea shot through her chest.

She gasped and stumbled up from the sofa, one hand gripping the door frame. She yanked the door open with too much force. The mesh slapped as she rushed inside.

She slammed it shut, breathing hard.

Just before she turned to go, she looked once more through the screen.

The yard was empty.

No eyes.

No movement.

Just blackness.

She didn't realize she was crying until she reached the bedroom and stood in the doorway. Joel snored softly on his side of the bed, unaware. She wiped her face, heart pounding.

Maybe she had imagined it. Maybe the shadows had played tricks on her. Whiskey and nerves. She hadn't eaten much at dinner. That could do it.

But no matter how she spun it in her head, nothing added up.

She slid into bed beside Joel, staring at the ceiling for a long time before sleep finally came in shallow, twitchy waves.

It wouldn't last.

******

Something woke her.

Not a sound at first, but the absence of it. That same unnatural stillness seemed to stretch and settle over the house like a shroud. Barbara opened her eyes and stared at the ceiling, unsure of how long she'd been asleep. The room felt colder than it should have been.

She turned her head toward the window. The curtains hung still. But something shifted outside, a shadow, brief and low, slipping past the frame.

She sat up, frowning. Joel breathed deeply beside her, one arm sprawled across the blanket, undisturbed.

There. A sound this time. Light. Unmistakenly intentional.

Tap. Tap.

Barbara held her breath.

It came again.

Not at the bedroom window, but from somewhere else in the house. Farther off. She slipped out of bed and crept toward the hallway, easing the door open just wide enough to slip through. The boards under her feet were cool and slightly warped with age, but she knew how to walk them quietly.

Another sound. This time at the front of the house.

Scratch. Tap. A pause. Then two more taps. Not like fingers. Not like claws either. Something in between. The pattern suggested curiosity, but not quite.

She stepped into the living room. The porch outside was dark. No streetlamp reached them this far out, and the porch light had burned out sometime last week. She had forgotten to replace it. Shadows bent oddly along the far wall, the little light that remained in the room catching on furniture and picture frames. The curtains in the kitchen hung undisturbed.

She reached for the light switch but stopped. Her instincts told her no.

Outside, near the porch, came a long exhale. Wet, low, almost thoughtful.

Barbara's stomach tightened.

She moved back into the hallway and turned toward the kitchen. The back of the house was darker. The only glow was from the microwave clock. She stared at the numbers and couldn't read them, her eyes refusing to adjust.

Something passed in front of the kitchen window.

A shape. Brief. Tall. It wasn't just moving by. It was looking in.

Barbara ducked behind the corner and pressed a hand to her chest. Her pulse thudded against her ribs. She felt foolish hiding in her own home but knew, deep down, that whatever was out there wasn't passing through. It was waiting for something.

A heavy thud hit the back porch.

She jumped. The screen door creaked softly, the sound of weight pressing against it. Not opening. Testing.

Another set of footsteps, slower. Moving across gravel.

Then silence again.

Barbara backed into the dining room, not wanting to wake Joel unless she had to. Maybe it was kids. Maybe someone was screwing around. But even as the thought came, she dismissed it. This wasn't the sound of kids on a dare. This was colder. It felt… sinister.

A single knock echoed from the front door.

She stared at it. The knock was soft. Rhythmic.

Knock. Knock.

Like it understood what the door was for.

Her mouth went dry. She moved toward it slowly, keeping out of view of the side window. She reached the peephole and almost didn't look through, afraid of what she might see.

She forced herself to.

Nothing.

She waited, holding her breath.

Then movement at the far edge of the yard. Not directly at the door. Something walked along the side of the house, low and slow.

She stepped back from the peephole and turned toward the hallway. She didn't make it two steps before something slammed against the side wall, hard enough to rattle a picture frame.

She bit down a scream and dropped to a crouch, heart hammering.

Something hit the screen door next. Not a full impact, but the sound of something dragging across it. A hand or claws or something worse.

Joel stirred.

Barbara crawled down the hall and slipped back into the bedroom. Joel sat halfway up, squinting.

"What are you doing?" he whispered.

"Something's outside," she whispered back. "More than one."

He rubbed his face. "What do you mean, something?"

"I saw eyes earlier. Now they're testing the house."

He blinked, clearly trying to shake off sleep. "Get the shotgun."

She was already moving.

From the hall, a low scrape echoed again, like nails along plaster.

Joel mumbled something under his breath and moved to the window, peeking through a slit in the curtain.

Barbara returned with the shotgun and handed it off.

"Should I call the sheriff?" she asked.

Joel shook his head. "No. I can handle it. We've got this and shells in the drawer. Anything out there would be stupid to try and come inside."

The porch outside was still dark.

They waited.

Barbara gripped Joel's arm.

Across the house, something hit the screen porch again.

Then silence.

Then running.

Four sets of footsteps, bare, powerful, fast, circled the house in unison. Gravel kicked up. Boards creaked near the porch. Something knocked over the trash bins. Then another figure rushed past the side window, too fast to see clearly.

Barbara flinched and grabbed Joel's sleeve.

"What do they want?" she whispered.

Joel didn't answer.

He stepped forward, opened the back door, and fired the shotgun straight through the screen. The blast shattered the quiet.

For a second, there was nothing.

Then a howl.

Not a dog. Not anything she had ever heard. It carried a sound inside it like broken glass and rage. One of them was hurt.

Joel stared toward the porch. "Is that a wolf?"

Barbara shook her head slowly, voice low. "If it's wolves, then they've learned to walk on two freakin legs."

The others responded with a deep, guttural rumble that passed through the wood floor like thunder.

Joel reloaded. "Go get the rifle. Load it and stay alert."

Barbara moved toward the hallway where she could see both ends of the house.

Something skittered onto the roof.

She looked up, staring at the ceiling as faint vibrations moved through the rafters. Whatever it was walked slowly, not trying to hide anymore. It moved like it had no fear of what might wait below.

Joel raised the shotgun again.

"Don't," Barbara said. "Not unless it comes through."

Outside, the gravel shifted again.

This time, they heard a dragging sound. Like something pulling its own leg. The one Joel hit.

Barbara turned back toward the living room window, where the glass had started to fog at the edges.

She walked closer.

There were handprints on the glass.

Two of them.

Impossibly large. Smudged at the fingertips. Long streaks where claws had scraped across the surface.

****

The house had gone still again, but it wasn't peaceful. Every wall, every floorboard seemed to listen.

Joel stood at the window with the shotgun tucked tight against his shoulder. Barbara moved through the kitchen, her hands steady despite the tremble she could feel under her skin. She found the rifle in the hall closet, where it had gathered dust behind a stack of boots and an old tackle box. She loaded it quickly, relying on memory. She paused once to listen.

The dragging sound had stopped.

When she stepped back into the living room, Joel acknowledged her but didn't speak. His jaw was set, eyes fixed on the fogged glass. The handprints were still there, just beginning to fade. She didn't need to be told they were watching.

Another knock. This time from the side door near the laundry room.

Three knocks.

Barbara raised the rifle. Her mouth was dry, and her tongue felt too thick. Joel motioned her to the hallway while he took a step toward the door.

The knock came again. But this time, it wasn't wood.

It was screen. Thin and metallic, the high-pitched rattle of claws tracing the mesh in a slow circle. The door handle twitched. Not hard. A test.

Barbara felt something shift behind her. She turned toward the back porch.

A faint scrape. Something brushing against wood and torn metal.

Her breath hitched.

Joel turned too, eyes narrowing.

The screen door was still hanging off its frame, warped and half-shattered from the shotgun blast. It swayed slightly now, nudged by something outside.

Barbara raised her rifle and stepped quietly toward the kitchen. The dark beyond the window was impenetrable. The only thing she could see was her own reflection.

The solid wooden back door held firm and steady.

Joel stepped beside her, shotgun already aimed.

They could hear movement just beyond it. Not footsteps

exactly. Weight shifting. Something dragging across the boards of the porch.

Then a breath.

Right on the other side. Wet. Slow. A sound like an animal savoring a scent.

Barbara watched the doorknob and froze when it twitched. Just a little. Just enough.

Joel gripped the shotgun tighter but didn't fire.

"If it comes through, then shoot," he said quietly. "Not before."

Barbara nodded.

They waited.

From the far side of the house came the sound of claws scraping down the siding. Another moved fast, skimming past the living room windows and toward the front door. Joel backed away from the kitchen. "They're feeling us out."

Barbara moved to the front. Her hand trembled now, but the rifle stayed level. She stopped near the entryway, where the dark pressed against the glass like smoke.

A shape paused just beyond the edge of the porch. Tall. Too tall. Its outline shifted, and she thought she saw a head tilt.

It stepped forward into view.

Her first instinct was to shoot, but Joel's words held her. The creature didn't charge. It didn't retreat. It stood just outside the line of shadow, eyes glowing faintly from beneath a sloping brow. Its arms hung low, and its chest moved with a slow, steady rhythm. It blinked once, then moved its head in a slow arc, as if scanning the house.

Joel appeared beside her and raised the shotgun again.

"Wait," Barbara whispered.

The creature stepped backward, melting into the dark.

For a moment, they heard nothing but their own breath.

Then a sharp cry broke the silence. Not a howl this time. A yelp, shrill and sudden.

And just like that, they were gone.

No footsteps. No rustling. Nothing.

Barbara stood frozen, watching the windows. The fog on

the glass cleared slowly, leaving only moisture and streaks behind.

Joel lowered the shotgun. "I think they got what they came for."

She took a deep breath she had been holding since it all began. "I hope so." Barbara replied. "I don't think I could take much more of this."

They checked the doors, reinforced the latches, pushed a chair under the front doorknob and stacked firewood behind the back one. Neither of them spoke.

An hour passed.

Then another.

They sat on the couch, side by side, weapons across their laps. The silence in the house felt thick, every creak, and shift of the wood carrying more weight than it should have.

Outside, the sounds of night returned one at a time.

Crickets first. Then the low hoot of an owl. Then a breeze moved through the trees, and it sounded like it always had.

But they didn't move.

They sat and listened, eyes fixed on the dark windows, too terrified to believe it was over. Too afraid to trust that whatever had come to their home had truly gone.

CHAPTER 12

The shrill buzz of Beretti's phone sliced through the dark. She groaned, one eye cracking open. The screen glowed on the nightstand. *Ben.*

She answered, voice thick. "Yeah?"

"Sorry to wake you," Ben said, low and serious. "Just got a call from Clay Darrow. Something happened out at his place. Sounds like Dogman trouble."

Beretti was already sitting up, pulling on her jeans. "We'll be ready in five."

She swung her feet to the floor and walked to the next bedroom, nudging Jacobi. "Up. Trouble."

He grunted, bleary but alert. "What kind?"

"Dogman kind."

Eight minutes later, they were out the door. No coffee. No real conversation. Just enough time to use the bathroom, grab jackets, and go. The air outside bit through fabric as they stepped onto the porch and headed to the SUV. Jacobi was behind the wheel of their SUV before he'd fully shaken off the sleep.

The drive took just under fifteen minutes. The sky was still black, a hint of gray smudging the eastern ridge. Clay's property sat quiet, porch light burning steady. As they pulled up, the old wooden boards creaked under his weight. Clay stood there with his shotgun cradled across his chest, eyes heavy but alert.

Ben stepped out of his cruiser first. "Mornin', Clay."

"Mornin'," Clay said, voice hoarse. "Looks like y'all brought backup."

"We figured it sounded urgent," Beretti said, stepping up beside him.

"Well, come on in."

Inside, the warmth of the house wrapped around them. "Jolene's still sleepin'," Clay said, catching Jacobi's glance down the hall. "Ain't told her yet. Figured best let her rest a bit longer."

They followed him into the living room. Clay lowered himself into the chair, shotgun resting across his knees, one hand still loose on the barrel.

"Got a call from my neighbor Ted 'bout an hour ago," he began, staring out the dark window. "Said he seen somethin' big. Thought it was a wolf, runnin' toward my place. Was talkin' real fast, like he'd spooked himself pretty good."

Beretti leaned forward slightly. "Ted was sure it was heading this way?"

"Near enough," Clay said. "Made me think it might be what I seen last week. I got up, left Jolene sleepin', grabbed my shotgun, and took up watch by the back door. Nothin' for a while, but then the motion light kicked on."

Jacobi rubbed his jaw. "How far does that light reach?" "Thirty feet, give or take. I looked out and just saw shadows at the edge. Might've been movement. Couldn't say for sure. But then I heard it. Heavy steps. Not runnin' exactly. Just... steady. Slow. Like it was makin' rounds."

He paused and glanced at the floor.

"I figured maybe it was circlin'. So I eased over to the front. Stared through the glass, had my hand on the lock. Thought about openin' it, but... somethin' in me said don't.

Real glad I listened."

Ben gave a small nod, quiet.

"I just stood there, listenin'. And I heard yippin'. But not like coyotes. I know what those sound like. This was different. High-pitched, but with this... cacklin' in it. Made the hair on my neck stand up. That's when I knew there was more than one."

Beretti's voice tightened. "From more than one direction?"

"Couldn't say for sure, but yeah. Sounded like it. Spread too wide for just one of 'em."

Jacobi let out a breath. "And after that?"

"I crept back to the kitchen. Looked toward the back door again. That's when I saw the muddy paw prints. On the tile. Some headin' in, some out. Door wasn't wide open, but it was unlatched."

His voice dropped a notch.

"I could've sworn I locked that thing. I always do. But I didn't hear nothin'. No creak, no latch click. It came in quiet."

"And left the same way," Ben said.

"Jolene never stirred," Clay added. "Still snorin' away when I checked. I ain't told her. Don't know how to. But now I'm thinkin' maybe it was a setup. Maybe me movin' to the front was just what it wanted."

Beretti gave a cautious nod. "Maybe."

Clay looked up. His face carried the burden of a man who'd seen something he couldn't shake.

"It was in my house. Even just for a second. And I didn't hear it."

Beretti stood. "We'll check the perimeter."

Clay dipped his chin slowly. "Mind keepin' this between us for now?

I'll tell Jolene. I just... need a minute to figure out how."

Ben put a hand on his shoulder. "Take your time."

Outside, Jacobi clicked on his flashlight and scanned the yard.

Motion lights blinked on as they moved. The front yard. The side of the house. The back door. They walked in a slow triangle, watching for anything, but beyond the splash of artificial light, it was nothing but dark, cold ground. No visible tracks.

"Only a slight wind," Jacobi mumbled. "Ground's soft. Should be something."

Beretti knelt by the edge of the porch, where the tiles turned to gravel. "It's too dark past the light spread. If there's tracks, they're just out of range."

Ben walked a slow lap around the back corner, stopping near the vegetable garden. "Might be better to check again after sunrise. Either way, sounds like the Dogman, or rather, Dogmen, came through here."

He walked back to the porch where Clay stood in the doorway, arms crossed.

"Might be a good time to visit family," Ben said. "Just for a few days. Let us handle this."

Clay didn't answer right away. He looked out toward the dark tree line at the edge of his property, where shadows still clung under the early light.

"Might not be a bad idea," he said at last. "Been meanin' to visit my sister anyhow. Guess now's as good a time as any."

"Good," Ben said. "I'll drive by your place and keep an eye

on it."

Jacobi stepped up beside them. "You said Ted called you? Does he border your land?"

"Yessir. Just over the ridge, northwest side. Ted Hoover."

Ben turned to Jacobi and Beretti. "If you two don't mind, head over and check on him. Maybe he got a good look at them."

Beretti gave a short nod. "We'll go now."

Clay stepped out onto the porch and leaned against the post, shotgun still tucked close.

"I been out here thirty-seven years," he said quietly. "Seen plenty that'll give you a chill. Even catchin' sight of that creature last week. But I ain't never felt watched like I did tonight."

Jacobi gave him a look. "We believe you."

Beretti added, "We'll get ahead of this."

Ben reached for the truck keys. "I'll circle the area. Keep an eye out for movement. You two check in with Hoover, then we regroup."

As they split up and headed to their vehicles, the first streaks of morning light were beginning to touch the tops of the trees, cold, and silver.

CHAPTER 13

Ted Hoover's place sat at the end of a narrow dirt road lined with leaning fences and draping oaks. Moss clung to the bark like the trees were trying to disappear. The deeper they drove, the quieter it got. Even the birds seemed to keep their distance.

Beretti slowed the SUV as a rusted mailbox came into view. It tilted like it had given up long ago. A wooden plank nailed to the fencepost read "NO TRESPASSING" in fading red paint. Below it, someone had scribbled in marker: "Unless You Brought Pie."

Jacobi raised an eyebrow. "You know this guy?"

Beretti nodded once. "In a manner of speaking."

They pulled up beside a weathered barn that looked like it was held together by habit and duct tape. A couple of chickens pecked at the dirt, flapping as the SUV came to a stop. One didn't bother moving. It stared at the vehicle like it had opinions.

Jacobi stepped out and glanced around. "Peaceful."

"Deceptive, alright," Beretti said.

The porch sagged under the weight of mismatched planters, rusty tools, and a faded taxidermy raccoon wearing a pair of sunglasses. Before they reached the steps, the screen door creaked open.

Ted Hoover stood barefoot, flannel pajama pants tucked into mismatched socks, and a long wool coat flapping around his legs. He held a spoon like it was a sidearm, his hair sticking up in wild tufts.

He squinted at Jacobi, then looked at Beretti. "Well now, who's this fella?" He pointed the spoon at Jacobi. "Your partner in bed, or partner in crime?"

Jacobi blinked once. "Neither. But nice to meet you too."

Beretti didn't flinch. "He's with me. Agents Beretti and Jacobi. We're here to talk."

Ted sniffed, then motioned toward himself. "Name's Ted. Most folks just call me Ted."

He stepped back and waved them both inside. "Don't touch the ceramic rooster. It's cursed. Swear on my mama's grave."

Jacobi glanced at Beretti with one eyebrow arched.

Inside, the place smelled like woodsmoke and leftover chili. A wood-burning stove clanked quietly in the corner. The walls were cluttered with maps, hunting photos, and a shelf full of VHS tapes. A shotgun rested in the corner by the fridge. Through the back screen door, chickens scratched in the dirt.

Jacobi looked around. "You always this welcoming?"

"You're lucky I like her," Ted said, dropping into a battered recliner. "I damn near shot ya at the mailbox."

Beretti stayed standing. "We heard you had some trouble this morning. Mind walking us through it?"

Ted rubbed his beard, then grabbed a thermos and poured steaming black coffee into a chipped mug. He drank first, then nodded.

"Started with the damn chickens. They don't raise hell like that unless somethin's out there fixin' to eat 'em. I figured fox, maybe a bobcat, could've been a damn raccoon hopped up on trash. Grabbed my light and my shotgun, stepped out."

Jacobi took out a small notebook. "What time was this?"

"A little before four. Sky was bright with moon, breath foggin' up in front of me like a freight train."

Beretti asked, "You hear anything besides the chickens?"

"No. Dead still before that. Then everything just... shifted."

Ted leaned forward, resting his elbows on his knees.

"You ever walk into a room and feel like somethin's watchin' you? That buzz in the air like right before a thunderhead busts open?"

Jacobi nodded. "Yeah."

"That's what it was like. The air felt weird. Heavy. I've lived here twenty-seven years, and I know what the night feels like. This was different."

Beretti's voice stayed calm. "What happened when you went outside?"

"I headed toward the coop. Light in one hand, shotgun in the other. The birds were flapping, slamming into the wire. I swung the beam around, and then I saw it."

Jacobi looked up from his notes. "Describe it."

Ted's expression shifted. Not fear exactly. More like unease that hadn't worn off yet.

"It weren't no bear. Weren't no bobcat. Sure as hell wasn't a Squatch. I seen those before, heard 'em too, off yonder past the ridge. This thing? It stood up tall. Real tall. Hunched some, like it was used to walkin' like that."

Beretti crossed her arms. "How close?"

"Fifteen, maybe twenty yards. Right near the fence line. I hit it full in the face with the light."

"And?"

Ted's voice lowered. "Had a muzzle on it. Like a dog, only meaner. Big ol' head. Eyes lit up red like they were burnin', not reflectin'. Thing didn't move at first, just stared like it was judgin' me."

Jacobi leaned forward. "Two legs?"

"Yeah. Then it dropped to all fours and ran. Damn fast. Moved like it had no weight. It went straight off toward my neighbor's place. I called him right after. Figured if I was seeing it, he might be next."

Beretti asked, "You ever seen anything like it before?"

"Never. And I've seen a lot of things in these woods. But this? This was unusual."

Jacobi nodded toward the shotgun in the corner. "You go after it?"

"I ain't stupid," Ted said. "I plopped down on that porch with the shotgun across my knees and waited for the sun like it owed me money."

Beretti studied him. "You said you've seen Sasquatch before."

"A few times. Mostly at dusk. They don't linger. Don't get close. They avoid trouble unless it comes knockin'."

"And this thing didn't?"

"No," Ted said. "This thing looked at me like I was the knock."

He got up and walked to the counter, pulled open a drawer, and returned with a hand-drawn map.

"This is the coop," he said, pointing. "It ran toward the

back treeline and into the woods. If it stayed on that line, it followed the old service trail, which runs straight toward Mill Creek. But it would've passed through Clay's land first, that's my neighbor. You can keep the map. I got plenty."

Beretti took the map. "Thanks."

Ted crossed his arms. "You plannin' to follow it?"

Jacobi said, "Soon as we have enough to work with."

"Bring fire," Ted said. "This thing didn't come from here. It brought somethin' with it. You ever step on land and feel it just... push back?"

Beretti met his eyes. "Yeah."

Ted exhaled through his nose. "Then you know."

They moved toward the door. Ted followed them out onto the porch.

"I know how I sound," he said, voice quieter now. "But don't let your training blind you. Just cause it don't make sense don't mean it ain't real."

Beretti turned back to him. "We believe you."

Ted nodded once, then looked at Jacobi. "You ever get

tired of being the sane one?"

Jacobi smiled faintly. "You'd be surprised."

They headed down the steps, past the chickens. One of them flapped at Jacobi's boots.

He gave it a wide berth. "That one's got murder in its eyes."

Ted grinned. "That's Delilah. She runs the place."

As they pulled away from the property, Beretti unfolded the map again, her fingers tracing the line between the two properties.

Jacobi glanced at her. "He only saw one."

"Doesn't mean there weren't others in the shadows," Beretti replied.

The trees lining the road held their secrets as Jacobi cast a glance in the rear mirror.

CHAPTER 14

Jacobi steered the SUV onto the main road heading back into Blackridge, eyes squinting against the rising winter light. Frost still clung to the edge of the windshield. In the passenger seat, Beretti's phone lit up and buzzed.

She answered with a clipped, "Beretti."

There was a pause as she listened, her posture stiffening. "Got it," she said, then hung up and turned to Jacobi.

"New plan," she said. "Ben just called. Another incident came in. Not far from Clay's place."

Jacobi didn't hesitate. He took the next turn and swung the SUV back around as Beretti tapped the address into the GPS. It led them further out the way they came, along a stretch of quiet land broken by a few scattered homes and barns.

When they arrived, the house looked old but well-kept. A long dirt driveway curved up past a row of young pine trees to a single-story home with a red tin roof and a deep porch that stretched around the back.

Beretti parked just outside the house and turned off the engine. The Lyons' home sat quiet and low against the edge of the woods, its screened porch sagging slightly at one corner. The back side of the house, visible from the drive, showed two screen doors barely hanging on.

Jacobi stepped out first, scanning the tree line.

"Anything?" Beretti asked.

"Nothing yet. Place feels still, but not in a good way."

They walked up to the porch. The front door opened before they could knock.

Joel stood in the entryway, still in the same clothes he'd worn the night before. His beard looked rougher, and his eyes were lined with exhaustion.

"I'm Joel Lyons," he said. "Come on in. Barbara's just inside."

He stepped aside. "Coffee's on if you feel like punishing

yourself."

Beretti gave him a polite greeting and stepped into the house. The air inside was warm and carried the faint scent of burnt dust, like the heater had been running nonstop.

Barbara sat on the far end of the couch, a thick blanket wrapped around her shoulders. Her hair was pulled back, though strands clung to her damp face. One leg bounced slightly, her fingers gripping the edge of the blanket. Her eyes found them but didn't stay. She looked worn thin, like someone still running on leftover adrenaline.

"Mrs. Lyons," Beretti said gently. "I'm Special Agent Beretti. This is Agent Jacobi. We understand you had a long night."

Barbara gave a quick, shallow reply, her hands moving restlessly. "I already went over everything with the sheriff. I did my best to explain it, but I can try again if you need to hear it from me."

Beretti remained standing. "Just walk us through what you remember. Start wherever feels right."

Barbara's eyes stayed fixed on the wall across from her. "I was out on the back porch. I always end my day there. One cigarette and a shot of whiskey before bed. Joel had already turned in. Everything was normal. I could hear frogs and insects. But then... it stopped. No wind. No sound. Just still."

Jacobi didn't speak, letting her continue.

"I saw eyes," she said. "They were low to the ground at first. Glowing orange-red. I thought deer, but they weren't spaced right. Too far forward. Not on the sides like a deer. And they weren't reflecting anything. They were just... glowing. Like coals."

She pulled the blanket tighter across her lap. "Then I saw more. Four sets total. One of them rose up like it had been crouching. And that was when it hit me. Bones shifting. Joints cracking into place. The sound crawled straight through me."

Her voice wavered but didn't stop. "I ran back inside and slammed the door. But they didn't try to get in. Not right away. They started circling. Scratching. Tapping. It felt... calculated. Like they wanted us to know they were there."

Joel's voice came from behind them. He leaned against the doorframe, arms folded. "They weren't just wild animals. I've lived in this house thirty years. I know the sounds things make out in the dark. This wasn't that. They had purpose."

Barbara gave a small shake of her head. "They were

playing with us. Hours of it. Joel fired once through the screen. We think he hit one. Something let out a noise. Not a dog. Higher. Sharp. And then they went quiet again."

"Did you see them leave?" Beretti asked.

"No," Barbara said, her voice barely above a whisper. "But I felt it. Like the air let go of me. I could breathe again."

Beretti turned to Joel. "Would you mind showing us around the property?"

Joel agreed. "Yeah. I'll show you what we saw. But Barb's staying inside."

"I'm not going outside," Barbara said immediately. "I sat with that rifle across my lap all night, watching shadows. Not again."

Beretti adjusted her coat and followed Joel through the house. They passed through the kitchen, where the inner wooden door remained closed. The back screen door behind it hung damaged, one corner cracked outward like something had hit it hard. Joel unlocked the wooden door and pushed it open slowly.

"The screen got busted," he said. "I fired through it last night. Heard something scream."

Jacobi stepped through after them. The porch creaked beneath their boots. Joel motioned toward the warped frame. "We forgot to latch it. Heard it shift while we were in the kitchen. That's when I knew it wasn't anything small."

Jacobi crouched beside the doorframe, examining the twisted wood and spotting black strands stuck in a split. He pulled on gloves, removed one gently, and placed it in an evidence pouch.

"Figured someone would want to take a look at that," Joel said.

They made their way around the house. The siding along the far wall was shredded in long arcs. At the edge of the property, one of the trash bins lay crushed and bent sideways.

Beretti moved slowly, eyes scanning the soil. She stopped near the side steps and crouched.

"Print," she said.

Joel stepped beside her. "Yeah, I saw that earlier. Nothing I've ever seen left tracks like that."

It was large. Toes long. Heel narrow. No sign of a tread.

Jacobi examined it closely but didn't comment.

Beretti stood again. "Mr. Lyons, we'd like to suggest you and your wife stay with friends or family. Just for a few days. Somewhere less isolated."

Joel's brow furrowed. "You think they'll come back?"

"We're doing everything we can to make sure that doesn't happen," Beretti said. "But these things weren't scared of you. That's what makes them dangerous."

Joel looked at the door again. At the siding. At the ground. "Yeah. No argument here."

"Do you want us to wait while you pack?" she asked.

Joel shook his head. "Thanks, but no. I've got the shotgun. We'll be fine."

Inside, Barbara remained on the couch. Her eyes were locked on the front window. Her fingers tapped the blanket, twitching in small bursts like her body refused to believe the danger had passed.

Outside, Beretti and Jacobi walked toward their SUV. The sky had started to lighten in the east, but the woods beyond the house still loomed in shadow.

Jacobi tilted his head. "So now we're looking at a pack of

at least four Dogmen. You ever handled that many at once?"

Beretti didn't break stride. "Nope. But I think we're about to."

CHAPTER 15

Beretti was behind the wheel, Jacobi silent beside her, when her phone buzzed in the cup holder.

She glanced down and saw Ben's name.

She put it on speaker. "Talk to me."

"Need you and Jacobi to head out to the local dump," Ben said. His tone was flat but tight at the edges. "Found something you're gonna want to see."

"Alright. Be there in ten."

She gave Jacobi a brief look, then flipped on the turn signal and took the next turn that led around the edge of town.

"No rest for the wicked, huh?" Jacobi said as he watched the frost-covered fields pass by.

The dump sat just outside Blackridge, tucked behind an old recycling center and a row of storage sheds. As they pulled up, Beretti spotted Ben standing near a weathered front-end loader. Beside him stood a thin young man who looked like he hadn't slept in days. He was rubbing one arm and shifting from foot to foot like he wanted to run but wasn't sure where to go.

Beretti stepped out of the SUV.

Ben gave a small smile. "Agents. This here's Lloyd Bingham."

The young man raised his head and acknowledged them, but didn't speak at first. His face was pale, skin shiny in places where sweat hadn't yet dried. His hair was damp and pressed flat against one side of his scalp, and he couldn't seem to keep his hands still.

Lloyd's voice came out high and uneven. "I didn't touch nothin'. Didn't go near it. I just saw 'em, that's it."

Beretti glanced at him calmly. "That's fine, Lloyd. We just want to hear what happened. From the beginning."

Lloyd sniffed, gave a jerky dip of his head, then spoke with no rhythm or pause.

"I got here this mornin' round seven. I'm the one who opens up. Boss is vacationing in Hawaii. Again. I checked the loader, topped it up with diesel, same as every other day. Nothin' weird. I was just doin' my job."

He took a breath that sounded like he hadn't realized he needed one.

"Got the machine goin', dropped the bucket down to start clearin' out the pile. First scoop I get, I go to turn like always, but I see somethin' hangin' over the edge. Legs. Looked like legs, anyway."

Beretti stayed quiet, letting him talk through it. "I stopped the machine right there. Let the bucket down real gentle and climbed out. Walked around just to be sure I wasn't imaginin' it. And yeah, there they were. Two bodies."

His voice dropped to almost a whisper.

"They looked like people. Almost. But not. Fur all over their legs, real coarse. Their feet were long and wrong lookin'. One had its mouth open. The teeth... they weren't right. Not like a person. More like a... like a coyote if you smashed its skull in and it got up anyway."

Jacobi shifted his weight slightly but didn't speak. "They were twisted up bad. Flies were everywhere. Loud.

Crawlin' on 'em like they'd been there all night."

Ben motioned toward him. "He didn't call anyone else. Straight to me."

Beretti looked at Lloyd. "Not even your boss?"

He shook his head. "No, ma'am. He doesn't take my calls when he is on vacation. Besides, I figured this wasn't the kinda thing I should be talkin' about to just anybody."

"Good instinct," she said. "Let's keep it that way. We'll arrange for someone to collect them as soon as possible. You don't need to do anything else."

Jacobi glanced toward the pile. "You didn't take any photos, did you?"

Lloyd shook his head quickly. "No, sir. Sheriff already checked. Said not to touch nothin' and I listened. Last thing I need is more trouble."

Lloyd swallowed hard but didn't look any calmer. "You think... they're the only ones?"

"We're working on that," Beretti said. "Right now, just keep this between us. Alright?"

He gave a quick shake of his head, like trying to clear it,

then said, "Mind if I go grab my bag from the office? I'm quittin' after this, 'cause the shit pay sure as hell ain't worth seein' one of those things again, not even if they're dead."

Ben gave him a pat on the shoulder. "Go on."

Lloyd turned and made for the squat cinderblock building near the gate. He didn't look back.

Once he was out of earshot, Ben motioned toward the rear of the loader. "Over here."

Beretti and Jacobi followed.

The smell hit before they saw them. It wasn't just the sour stink of garbage, but something fouler layered beneath. Dense, rancid, and unmistakably tied to death. It clung in the throat like wet ash. Trash shifted in shallow piles along the dirt and flies swarmed in and out of torn bags and cracked containers.

There, amongst the rotting garbage, were the bodies.

Two of them lay twisted and still, their long limbs tangled in the debris, blood-matted fur clinging to slack muscle. Their faces looked misshapen, with muzzles too broad, jaws warped open, and teeth jagged and irregular. One had what looked like a wound at the base of its skull, while the other's chest was sunken inward.

Jacobi crouched. "Dogmen."

Beretti gave a calm confirmation. "Affirmative."

Ben looked from one body to the other, his mouth tightening. "First time I've ever seen one of these." His eyes narrowed. "Ugly bastards, aren't they?"

Jacobi didn't respond.

Ben took a step back and looked around the area. "You think it was townsfolk who dumped them here? Or something else? Like a Sasquatch?"

Beretti shook her head. "I doubt it was people. If a human actually managed to kill two Dogmen, they wouldn't just leave them here. They'd take something. Teeth. Hide. Something to mount or brag about. These weren't killed for sport or trophy."

She gestured toward the crushed skull and the sunken chest. "More likely a Sasquatch killed them. Given the damage, the strength behind it, and where they ended up? Makes more sense. Whoever did this knew this dump stinks worse than anything. Probably didn't even need to come all the way in. Just smelled it from the tree line and knew it's where humans leave what they don't want."

Jacobi studied the bodies for a long moment. "That's exactly what it looks like."

Ben squinted toward the treeline. "How do we even know how many we're dealing with?"

Jacobi didn't look up. "We just came from the Lyons' place. Barbara said she saw four sets of eyeshine out there last night."

Ben frowned. "You think these could be two of them?"

Beretti stepped forward. "Unlikely. But not impossible."

She crouched down, studying one of the corpses. "What matters is we now know the Sasquatch are aware. And they're not just watching anymore, they're acting."

Jacobi kept his eyes on the treeline. "If the Squatch are already out here cleaning up, where do we fit in?"

Beretti didn't hesitate. "We're here to keep people from getting caught in the middle of a turf war. Our job is limiting the damage."

Ben acknowledged her and glanced down again. "So what do you want to do with them?"

"Jacobi, can you call it in?" Beretti asked.

Jacobi gave a simple yes and walked a few paces away, phone already coming out of his coat.

Beretti turned to Ben. "FBI will send a van. No lights. No markings. Fast and quiet. They'll be gone before the next shift shows up."

Ben scratched at the back of his neck. "Sounds about right."

Jacobi returned a minute later, tucking the phone away. He looked down once more at the bodies. "Two down. No idea how many left."

Beretti didn't answer.

She didn't need to.

They all knew there were more out there.

CHAPTER 16

THE DOGMAN

It watched from the hollowed base of a tree, breath low, chest still. The cold earth beneath its belly cooled the blood that had started to warm again. It needed that stillness. Needed the patience.

The stink had been thick for half a mile. Clung to the air like decay. Damp hair. Wet leaves. The sour stink of sweat. And beneath it, that sweet rot. The scent of the tall ones. The walking stench. The Sasquatch.

Its lip curled, exposing yellowed teeth slick with saliva. It hated the smell. All Dogmen did. It clung to the throat, coated the tongue, and crept into the sinuses. These things stank of rot and rain and dirt. Dumb, heavy beasts stomping through the forest as if they owned it. Always lumbering. Always noisy.

And stupid. This one especially.

It had followed the scent for hours. A young one, judging by the clumsiness of its trail. The breaks in the undergrowth were wide, the footfalls uneven. No real caution. No wariness. Just a stupid, towering pile of flesh wandering too far from whatever pathetic nest it had crawled out of.

The Dogman shifted, one clawed hand anchoring its body to the roots. Every muscle coiled. It wanted the kill. Not out of hunger, but out of disgust. The stench, the ignorance, the arrogance of it all. Sasquatch were not predators. They were watchers, cowards, heavy-legged observers who barely defended what was theirs.

It moved again, silent as fog. Through the brambles, up the ridge, over the slick of wet rock and fallen pine needles. The Sasquatch was close. Still unaware. The scent was fresher now, and below it.

The Dogman climbed.

Its body slid up the tree with ease, claws sinking into bark like hooks, legs folding tight beneath it. It climbed high. Higher than most things would risk. It clung there, unmoving, nose twitching, ears swiveling to the smallest noise.

Below, the Sasquatch appeared.

Young. Maybe five feet tall, barely old enough to have strength in its limbs. Its arms were too long for its body. The hair patchy in places, dark and matted with creek water. It stopped by the stream, the one with the twisted alder roots and cold runoff from the ridge. Bent to drink. Clumsy again. Loud.

The Dogman snarled in silence. The sound stayed in its chest.

So stupid. So slow. It didn't smell the danger. Didn't feel the quiet closing in. It drank like the forest belonged to it, unaware of the death above its head.

The Dogman's jaw dripped. Not from hunger. From anticipation.

It waited. Still. Breath controlled. It would not pounce yet.

Let it turn.

Let it look away.

A bird called in the distance. The wind shifted.

Now.

The Dogman leapt.

It hit the juvenile Sasquatch with the force of a falling tree. The impact cracked bone. The Sasquatch screamed once, high and broken, before the Dogman's jaws locked onto the base of its neck.

The bite crushed vertebrae. The scream ended. Legs twitched but no longer held weight.

The Dogman fell with it, pinning the body to the mud.

It didn't hesitate. Claws raked through the chest, shredding muscle and hair. Blood sprayed across the rocks. Its hind legs kicked, talons tearing through the abdomen like wet paper. Guts spilled. The Sasquatch spasmed once more, a dying reflex.

The Dogman breathed hard, saliva and blood dripping from its face. The smell was unbearable now, even worse than before, but it kept going, clawing through bone, rending muscle, until the ribcage sagged inward like a collapsed shelter.

It stood.

The body twitched again.

A final insult.

The Dogman raised a clawed foot and slammed it down on the skull.

Silence returned.

No birds. No squirrels. Even the stream seemed slower now.

It dragged the corpse by the ankles, away from the stream, away from the bloodied rocks. Deeper into the underbrush where the soil turned loamy and dark. It used its hands to dig, fast and efficient, making a shallow pit just wide enough. The smell was thick. Flies gathered already.

Stink-wings, the Dogman called them. Carrion eaters. Always late to the feast but eager.

It shoved the Sasquatch into the pit. Blood soaked the earth. The flies surged. It covered the body with leaves and dirt, pressed it flat, then stood over it for a moment, listening.

Still nothing.

Then it heard something.

Not far. Approaching footsteps. Lighter. Quicker.

Hesitant.

A hairless one.

Its ears twitched.

Another sound followed. Pads on dirt. A sniff. A low growl.

A canine.

The Dogman went still.

The stink of the hairless one and its loyal friend offended its senses. The sounds of breath not held right. The hairless one was oblivious. The canine was more alert.

It didn't move.

It would not give itself away.

Not yet.

The Dogman slunk backward, into the thicker brush, into the rot and moss where its coat blended with the dark. Its chest rose and fell once. Then again. Slowly now. Quietly.

It would wait.

Watch.

CHAPTER 17

The diner sat just off the main road, tucked between a bait shop and a hardware store with sun-faded signage. A red "OPEN" sign on the door swung gently in the breeze. Inside, the linoleum floor bore the wear of decades of boots and muddy soles, and the air smelled like grease and maple syrup.

Beretti and Jacobi took a booth near the window. A waitress who looked like she'd been there forever poured two mugs of steaming coffee without a word. The place was quiet, the energy slow. Locals hunched over their plates, a radio near the kitchen whispered country tunes.

Jacobi sipped his coffee and smiled. "Burnt and bitter. Just how I like it."

Beretti kept her eyes on the window, hands wrapped around the mug. Outside, the mist was beginning to lift from the trees, and the ridgeline slowly came back into view.

They'd ordered eggs, toast and hash. Nothing fancy. Just fuel.

Jacobi finally broke the silence. "Each of them only saw one. Clay. Deborah. The kids at the bbq. But Ted, he said he heard more than one but didn't actually see them."

Beretti didn't look at him. "Barbara saw four sets of eyes."

"And now two bodies dumped at the edge of town," Beretti added.

She set the mug down and leaned back slightly. "We don't know how many are out there, or how many the Sasquatch have already come across."

Jacobi exhaled deeply and rested his forearms on the table, eyes fixed on the condensation running down his glass.

Beretti's gaze followed the waitress as she filled two water jugs at the next table. "We can't stop what's happening out there, but we can make damn sure the townsfolk aren't dragged into it."

****

They ate quietly for a while. Just the clink of forks, the scrape of plates, and the low murmur of conversation from two booths over. The quiet was comfortable until Jacobi broke it.

"You planning to see anyone else while you're here?"

Beretti didn't look up. "No."

"Not even friends? Family?"

"I visit my uncle once a year. That's enough."

Jacobi didn't push. "Fair enough."

He took another bite, then set his fork down. "You don't talk about this place much."

Beretti shrugged. "Not much to say. It is my past."

The door opened behind them, and the bell above it gave a sharp jingle. Cold air swept in, followed by the scrape of boots across tile.

"Well, well. Look who crawled out of D.C. and remembered this place exists."

Beretti's shoulders stiffened. She didn't turn.

Jacobi did. A tall woman with a thick braid over one shoulder and a weathered coat stood near their booth. Her voice carried easily, but it wasn't friendly.

"Mara," Beretti said flatly.

"Still remember my name?" the woman replied. "Guess you haven't forgotten everything."

Jacobi looked between them. "Cousin?"

"On her mother's side," Mara said. "The side she doesn't talk to anymore."

Beretti kept her tone even. "Not here."

Mara ignored her. "We hear about you. Coming to town. Visiting your uncle. But never stopping by the river. Never asking about your mother's people. Never calling when it matters."

Jacobi sat forward. "That's enough."

Mara's eyes snapped to him. "Who's this pretty boy? Another fed?"

Beretti touched Jacobi's arm lightly. "It's okay."

Mara's voice lowered. "We buried Auntie Leni last year.

You didn't even call. She was blood. Sat beside your mom at every council fire. Told stories about you like you were her own. But I guess that's just another chapter you decided didn't matter anymore."

Beretti stayed still, quiet.

"You think showing up in this town once a year for your uncle makes it right? The rest of us are still here. Still trying to hold the threads together. And you... you just walk away and don't look back."

Jacobi stood. "You've said your piece."

Mara looked at Beretti one last time. "You don't even smell like home anymore."

She turned and left. The bell rang again as the door swung shut behind her.

Silence settled in like dust.

Jacobi sat slowly. "You okay?"

Beretti didn't speak at first. Her eyes stayed on the empty mug in front of her.

"She's not wrong." Beretti said quietly.

"About what?" Jacobi asked.

Beretti took a breath. "I stopped going to see that side of the family. After my mom died. I told myself it was easier. Cleaner. No ghosts to stir up."

Jacobi didn't respond. Just waited.

"I visit Ben. That's it."

She picked up her fork, then set it back down.

Jacobi gave her the space.

The check came, and before Beretti could reach for it, Jacobi dropped a bill on the table and pushed the slip toward the edge.

"I've got this one."

She gave him a look, but didn't argue.

They left the diner and stepped into the cold. The wind had picked up, carrying with it a damp, earthy bite that hinted at more cool weather on the way.

As they reached the SUV, Jacobi spoke again.

"You don't owe anyone an explanation. But you don't

have to carry all of it alone either."

Beretti opened the driver's side door and paused.

"I've been carrying it for a long time," she said. "It's mine to bear."

Jacobi didn't argue. He just got in.

"So, where to now?" he asked.

"I've been thinking about someone who might know a thing or two about the history between the Dogmen and the Sasquatch. Figured I'd check if he still hangs out at the same spot."

Jacobi gave a slight shrug. "Can't hurt."

They pulled out of the lot without another word.

CHAPTER 18

The bar didn't have a name on the door, just a warped license plate nailed to the siding and a single yellow bulb buzzing faintly above the frame. Beretti pulled into the lot, and parked. The place was quiet. A single motorcycle leaned beside a rust-specked pickup.

Jacobi squinted through the windshield. "This the spot?"

Beretti nodded. "Elijah Greyfeather drinks here most afternoons. Sits near the back where he can watch the door."

"You sure he'll talk?"

"I'm not sure of anything with him. But he knows the stories. My mother used to say he remembered things others had forgotten."

They stepped inside. The room held the kind of stale warmth that came from years of closed windows and quiet drinking. Walls stained a shade darker than they were painted, lined with faded photos no one looked at anymore. A jukebox sat silent in the corner, its casing scratched and dull, like it hadn't worked in years. The floor creaked underfoot, but the bartender didn't look up.

Elijah sat in the last booth, alone. A glass of amber liquor rested near his hand. He wore a camo jacket over a dark shirt, his long gray hair tied back. His skin was leathery from sun and wind, eyes still sharp despite the whiskey.

Beretti approached without hesitation.

"Elijah."

He avoided looking up. Just reached for his glass, took a sip, then glanced over.

"Well I'll be damned," he said. "You're the Beretti girl."

She gave a nod. "That's right."

"You used to come runnin' around your daddy's boots like you owned the place." He gave a dry chuckle, voice just a bit thick. "Spirited. That's what folks used to say."

Beretti smiled faintly. "You served with him."

Elijah nodded. "Your father came in green, fresh outta

Fort whatever, and they handed him to me like a damn paperweight. I taught him how to keep his head low and listen to the woods."

Jacobi hovered near the edge of the booth. "Mind if we sit?"

Elijah's eyes shifted to him, sizing him up in a single glance. "You're not family."

"Special Agent Jacobi," he said, calm but clear.

Elijah looked back to Beretti. "You brought a fed to my booth?"

"I brought someone I trust," she said. "We're not here to stir anything up. We just need to ask you something."

He leaned back, picked up his glass again. "Well go on, then."

Beretti met his eyes. "We're here to talk about Sasquatch. And Dogmen."

Beretti answered, "We work for the FBI. Our job is to handle any wayward cryptids before they become a problem for people."

Elijah stared at her, then gave a slow grin. "Should've

known. It's in your blood."

"There's a war goin' on right now," he said slowly. "Figured that's why you're here."

Jacobi leaned forward slightly. "You've seen something?"

"I've seen enough," Elijah replied. His voice slurred just faintly at the edges now, thick with whiskey and memory. "But it ain't about what I saw. It's what I remember bein' told."

Jacobi replied. "Can you tell us what you know?"

He ran a finger around the rim of the glass.

"My people don't call them Sasquatch or Dogmen. Those are white-man names. The first, the tall ones, quiet and strong, we called the Watchers. The other ones, the ones that run fast and tear things apart for the fun of it, we called Bone-Mouths."

Beretti folded her hands on the table. "Have they always been here?"

Elijah shook his head slowly. "Nah. Not both. The Watchers, yeah. They been here a long time. Came after the fire, long before memory. They watched. They waited. Never spoke like we do, but they understood."

He pointed vaguely with his glass. "Stayed in the high ridges. The quiet places. Lived low and slow."

Jacobi asked, "And the Dogmen?"

"They came up from the south. Swamps. Shadows. Old rot and bad air. My grandmother's grandmother used to say you could smell 'em before you saw 'em. Smelled like spoiled meat and blood gone wrong."

He gave a short laugh that didn't hold humor. "They didn't build nothin'. Didn't plant. Just took. Always takin'."

Beretti kept her eyes on him. "When did the fighting start?"

Elijah's fingers moved along the table's edge. "Hard to say. First, there was distance. They kept to their places. Then the forest changed. Fires came. Roads got cut. Noise. The Bone-Mouths pushed north. Something got crossed. Maybe one of 'em took a young one. Maybe just wandered too far."

His voice dropped.

"The Watchers responded. Quick. One Bone-Mouth got strung up in a pine. Left there for days. Message was clear."

Jacobi frowned. "Territorial?"

Elijah shrugged. "Sure. But it was more than that. Bone-Mouths didn't take the warning. They don't read signs. Don't know what trees mean or stones stacked on trails. Next thing we know, there's more blood. Then it just kept goin'. Quiet battles. One side pushin', the other holdin' ground."

Beretti leaned in. "And now?"

"They're back at it. Watchers ain't gonna run. But they won't wait around neither. Not if the Bone-Mouths keep movin' closer to people."

Jacobi's tone was careful. "We found two bodies out at the local dump. Torn up bad. We think the Sasquatch killed them."

Elijah didn't blink. "Sounds about right. They left 'em where it stinks so no one would mistake the point. Trash for trash. That's how they see it."

Beretti asked, "Are there more coming?"

"There always are," Elijah said. "Bone-Mouths travel in packs when they can. If you saw two, there's more nearby. The Watchers know it too."

Jacobi rubbed the back of his neck. "So the Sasquatch are trying to contain it."

"They're tryin' to survive," Elijah replied. "Same as they always have. But if the Bone-Mouths get too daring, people are gonna pay for it."

Beretti studied his face. "You've seen one. A Sasquatch."

"Years ago. Elk huntin' west of the ridge. Felt like I was bein' followed. Turned, and there it was. Bigger than any man. Just watchin'. Didn't move. Didn't blink. Then it was gone."

Jacobi asked, "And the Dogmen?"

Elijah's voice dropped even lower. "You don't see them unless they want you to. And if they want you to, it's too late."

Beretti stood. "Thank you."

Elijah lifted his glass in her direction. "You wanna keep folks alive, stay between them and the fire."

"We're trying," she said as she exited the bar.

Outside, the air had cooled. The wind came off the trees with a rustle like whispers.

Jacobi looked out toward the tree line. "So what now?"

Beretti opened the SUV door and glanced back once toward the bar.

"We need to stop it before it reaches the town.," she said.

CHAPTER 19

The afternoon light spilled across the ridge trail in broken stripes, sliding through the canopy like liquid gold. Shana Voss walked at a steady pace, boots brushing fallen needles, her Doberman, Dallas, moving a few steps ahead.

The woods were quiet this time of day, not empty, just resting. She liked it that way. Mornings were for noise, for caffeine and emails. Afternoons, especially ones like this, were for peace and clearing her mind.

Dallas stayed just ahead, ears swiveling, her body loose but alert. The trail dipped and curved, bending around a thick cluster of fir trees. A mix of evergreens and bare, leafless trunks lined the ridge like quiet watchmen. Somewhere behind them, a bird trilled, then stopped short.

Shana rubbed her arms, breathing deep. "Cold's clinging

on longer than usual," she mumbled.

Dallas didn't turn, but her ears twitched at the sound of her voice. They always walked together. Ritual more than routine. After eight years, they moved like one.

Dallas veered ahead, paws silent over the cold ground. She disappeared around a bend where the trail narrowed between two slanted rock shelves. It wasn't unusual. Dallas always scouted ahead. Always returned within moments.

Shana kept walking. Her boot clipped a root, and she stumbled slightly but caught herself, huffing a soft laugh. The cold made everything feel heavier. Slower.

"Don't go too far girl," she called, her voice steady.

Silence.

She slowed, frowning. No tags jingled. No soft footfalls padding back.

"Dally?"

Still nothing.

The trees grew a little denser here. She could still see the trail, but it narrowed ahead, shadowed by old trunks and clusters of dense undergrowth. The air felt different. Not the kind of stillness that calms, but the kind that builds behind closed doors before a storm.

Shana took two steps forward and paused.

A branch cracked.

Not far.

Straight ahead.

She didn't call out again. Her body moved before her brain caught up, scanning the trees, the ground, listening for movement. Something about the noise didn't match the usual rhythm of deer or squirrel.

"Dallas?" Her voice was lower now.

A shape stepped onto the trail.

Shana froze.

It wasn't Dallas. It wasn't anything she expected to see.

The figure that emerged from the trees was tall. Its shoulders nearly brushed the hanging limbs of a bent fir, and its body moved with a coiled, unnatural fluidity. It walked upright, chest rising and falling, each step slow and steady. Fur as black as midnight covered its limbs in matted ridges, slick in places like it had dragged itself through something wet. Its arms were long, too long, ending in hands like a racoon that curled into claws the size of carving knives.

It stared at her. Intensely.

Eyes deep-set and yellow, rimmed in red. Muzzle slightly open. The breath that escaped from between its teeth was damp and warm enough to steam in the cold.

Shana didn't scream. She couldn't.

Her feet backed up on instinct, one step, then another. The thing took a step forward. The sound of its foot hitting the trail was muffled, as if the very air had gone rigid in anticipation.

"Oh God, oh God, oh God."

Instantly, it closed the distance between them with incredible speed. Shana turned, stumbling backward, barely catching herself. She didn't have time to think, only to react, arms up, breath torn from her lungs as the creature collided with her.

She hit the ground hard, her shoulder catching the edge of a root, pain blooming white across her ribs. The Dogman loomed above her, breath thick, teeth exposed, one clawed hand braced against the dirt beside her face.

It reeked of wet dog, decay, and something sulfurous, like rotten eggs left too long in the heat.

A snarl ripped from its throat. Saliva dripped from its maw, strands catching in the light as it raised its other arm.

A blur of motion slammed into its side.

Dallas.

The Doberman crashed into the creature's ribs at full speed, teeth locked onto its neck. The momentum knocked the Dogman off-balance, and they rolled together, snarling, twisting.

Shana scrambled back, gasping, hand pressed to her ribs.

Dallas was feral, snapping, biting, every muscle straining as she clung to the monster's throat. The Dogman slammed its back against a tree, throwing its weight hard, trying to dislodge her.

With a final wrench, it grabbed Dallas by the scruff and hurled her across the trail.

She hit the ground with a sickening thud, yelped once, and rolled.

The Dogman didn't follow. It turned, crouched low, and bounded into the trees, vanishing in two strides.

The woods snapped back to calm as if nothing had occurred.

Shana crawled toward Dallas, who was already pushing herself upright, slow, but alive. Her eyes were wide, panting hard and a cuts near her muzzle and neck dripped blood slowly.

Shana cupped her face and gave her a kiss on the head. "Good girl. Good girl."

Her hands trembled. Her heart thudded so loudly she thought it might drown out everything else.

The trees ahead stood quiet.

The trail behind waited, empty.

They couldn't stay here.

Not a second longer.

CHAPTER 20

An hour later, the trailhead was taped off. Deputies posted up the markers while Ben, Jacobi and Beretti stepped onto the scene.

Scraped pine needles lined the edge of the trail, a torn piece of jacket caught on a low branch nearby. Every detail pointed to sudden movement. Disorientation. Panic.

Beretti knelt beside a deep gouge in the soil. "She fell here. There's a heel mark, and drag behind it. She tried to push off, but it took her down before she got far."

Jacobi pointed further along the trail. "She turned to run. It came after her from behind."

Ben crossed his arms, eyes scanning the treeline. "So where did it come from?"

Beretti stood and moved slowly up the trail, gaze fixed to

the ground. "Not from behind her. Look at the spacing. Footprints, long stride. It was already ahead, waiting."

She walked a few more paces before stopping at a narrow break in the brush.

"This is where it came through," she said, crouching slightly. "It stepped out just before she reached this spot. She must've seen it and turned back. That's when it chased her."

Jacobi came up beside her. "Aggressive. Territorial."

Beretti ducked through the opening in the undergrowth without another word.

Ben and Jacobi followed, their sidearms drawn and held low. The woods swallowed them quickly, and the air turned colder beneath the thick canopy. Every step was soft, the forest floor a blanket of old needles and rotting leaves.

Beretti slowed.

About thirty yards in, there was a mound near the base of a tree. Pine needles had been scattered over the top, but the dirt underneath looked recently disturbed. Uneven. Hasty.

She crouched.

The smell hit first. Urine, strong and acrid. Beneath that,

blood.

She brushed some of the cover away and revealed tangled reddish-brown hair, soaked and matted. A shoulder. A narrow back.

Jacobi joined her and helped clear more dirt. Together they dug a little deeper, exposing the full shape.

Ben took a half-step forward. "Is that...?"

Beretti uncovered more. The body was about five feet long, humanoid but not human. Broad hands. Long limbs. Slack features twisted in death. Its chest and abdomen had been torn open. Deep slashes crossed its face, including two raking down both eyes.

Jacobi crouched beside her. "Young Sasquatch." Beretti nodded. "Killed recently. The cuts are fresh."

Ben turned his head slightly. "The smell... it pissed on it?"

"Claimed it," she said. "This wasn't random. It was a kill. Then a message."

Jacobi kept his voice low. "You think it meant to eat it?" Beretti looked at the wounds. "Maybe. But it buried it like a predator caches food. Or maybe to keep others from taking it."

Ben looked around and stepped away from the tree. "There are drag marks."

He followed the trail about twenty feet and stopped. "Here. This is where it happened."

He gestured to a scuffed patch of dirt, broken branches, and a pool of dark blood. "It killed it here. Then dragged the body over and dug the grave."

Beretti watched him a moment, then looked back toward the mound.

Ben peered back in the direction of the trail. "Would they come for it? The Sasquatch, I mean."

"No," Beretti said. "Not now. Not with that scent all over it. This thing's been marked. Defiled. They'll leave it."

She rose, pulling out her phone. "I'll call ASIC Ward. He'll send a recovery team. No way we leave this here."

Jacobi stood slowly. "You think this is the first one it's killed?"

"No," she said. "Just the first we've found."

They fell quiet as the light began to shift. The trees held still. There were no sounds beyond them. No birds. No breeze.

Just the thick smell of blood and urine clinging to the air.

Beretti gave the clearing one last look, then turned toward the path. "This changes everything."

Ben didn't speak.

They started walking towards the trail, as Beretti exhaled and stretched her back. "I need to grab some wipes when we get back to the SUV. I smell like piss."

Jacobi pulled out his phone. "Want the GPS coordinates?"

"Yeah," she said. "Send them to me so I can get them to ASIC Ward."

He tapped a few times, then gave a short nod. "Sent."

Beretti gave him a quick glance. "Thanks."

Jacobi didn't say anything else. Neither did she. They just kept walking, the woods closing quietly behind them.

CHAPTER 21

The automatic doors slid open with a soft hiss just as Shana Voss stepped out of the hospital lobby, her movements stiff from bruised ribs and a sore shoulder. She blinked in the low evening light.

At her side was a woman in her fifties, walking close. Her mother. She looked shaken but composed, eyes sharp with protective energy. She let Shana lead.

Ben Beretti stood waiting near the sidewalk. Jacobi leaned on the fender of the SUV while Nicole lingered by the passenger door. When Shana noticed them, she stopped.

"Sheriff," she said, voice tired but steady. "Figured someone would come around."

Ben stepped forward with a calm, professional nod. "Didn't want to crowd you earlier. Just wanted a few minutes of your time before you headed out."

She shifted the jacket under her arm. "That's fine. I'm not going far. My sister's at the vet with Dallas. They're patching her up now."

"Brave dog," Ben said. "She saved your life."

Shana's throat bobbed with a swallow. "Yeah. She did."

Jacobi came closer but stayed quiet. Beretti did the same, letting Ben take the lead.

Ben kept his voice low. "Can you walk us through it? Just the basics."

Shana nodded. "I don't know what it was. I know what it looked like, but it shouldn't exist. It had the head of a wolf, but it moved like a man. Nothing should move that fast."

She drew in a breath. "Dallas had trotted ahead around a bend, like she always does. The air felt off somehow. Then this thing stepped onto the trail and just stood there, staring. I turned to run and I think I tripped. Next thing I knew, it was on top of me."

Her voice caught. "It was about to strike when Dallas slammed into it. She saved me." A tear slid down her cheek.

She looked away for a moment. "It threw her off and took

off into the woods. Thank God."

"I don't think I'll ever walk that trail again. I can't stop seeing its face."

Ben asked quietly, "Do you have any injuries?" "Yeah. Just bruising. My shoulder and ribs took the worst of it. Dallas has a few cuts and some bruising too. But she's tough. She'll be okay. She's the best dog I've ever had. She's getting a big-ass steak for dinner tonight."

Her mother stood beside her, hand resting lightly on her back, silent through the exchange.

Beretti stepped forward. "You heading to the vet now?"

"Yeah."

Ben handed her a card. "If anything else comes back to you, even a small detail, call us."

Shana took it and slid it into her jacket pocket. "I will." She turned to go, then hesitated. "Whatever that thing was, Sheriff... it doesn't belong here. Hell, it doesn't belong anywhere."

Ben didn't speak. He held her gaze and gave a quiet nod. Shana and her mother walked toward the car.

The three of them stood in silence, watching them go. Beretti finally let out a breath. "Let's hope that's the worst of it."

No one answered.

None of them believed it was.

CHAPTER 22

The wind had picked up as they stood outside the SUV, watching the two women drive away. Ben leaned against the hood of his cruiser, arms crossed. Jacobi stood beside him while Beretti zipped up her coat.

"We need to talk about the town," Beretti said, glancing toward the street. "People need to know what's out there. Well, within reason, anyhow."

Ben arched an eyebrow. "You want me to tell them what exactly? That there's a monster in the woods?"

"Not the truth. Not fully," Jacobi said. "But we can't keep it quiet anymore. There have been too many incidents."

Ben shifted his weight, one boot scuffing against the pavement. "What are you thinking?"

"A predator bulletin," Beretti said. "Something like unusual predators have been seen in the area. Warn them to stay inside from dusk till dawn and don't go hiking alone. Keep animals secured. That sort of thing. Just keep it simple so the majority listen, and do the right thing."

Ben rubbed his moustache slowly, thinking it through. "We've had the teens out on the outskirts get mauled, a Dogman enter Clay's home, a pack destroy someone's porch, two corpses dumped at the landfill, and now Shana…"

Jacobi finished it. "And a Sasquatch corpse buried like food. You don't need to tell them everything. Just enough to be cautious."

Ben exhaled through his nose. "Yeah. It's getting worse."

"They'll trust you," Beretti said. "If it comes from you, they'll listen. Well, most of them and that is the best we can hope for."

Ben gave a slow nod. "All right. I'll put together a statement. Nothing fancy. Text alert, bulletin board, maybe a call-in spot on the local station."

"Make it clear that no one should try to hunt them," Jacobi added. "You know there'll be at least one guy out there with a six-pack and a rifle."

"No doubt. I'll stress they are dangerous and unpredictable," Ben said. "No hunting. Call it in if they see anything."

Beretti pulled her keys from her coat pocket. "We'll head back to your place. Leoni still cooking?"

"I would imagine so," Ben said. "I'll meet you both there after I get this sent out."

Jacobi nodded. "We'll be waiting."

Ben climbed into his cruiser and started the engine. The headlights lit up the side of the building before he turned out toward the main road.

Beretti looked over at Jacobi. "Come on. Let's move."

****

The porch light cast a warm glow as the wind stirred the chimes, their hollow notes echoing across the yard. Beretti led the way up the steps and unlocked the door. Inside, the rich scent of roasted vegetables, garlic, and seared chicken greeted them. After the day they'd had, it was a welcome comfort.

She slipped off her boots and hung her coat on the rack by the door, smoothing it flat before stepping inside.

Jacobi followed, his eyes scanning the cozy kitchen and warm wooden interior. Whiskey barked once from under the dining table before trotting over to greet them, tail wagging. Wink stayed curled on the rug, lifting his head but not bothering to move.

Leoni's voice came from the kitchen. "You're late."

Beretti smiled. "You're early."

Leoni looked up, wiping her hands on a towel. "I started dinner after Ben called. Figured you'd be dragging your feet."

Jacobi offered a small wave. "Smells amazing."

Leoni eyed him with amusement. "You always this polite?"

"He tries," Beretti said, moving toward the back door to let the dogs out.

Leoni grinned. "Ben said he'd be home in twenty minutes. You two hungry?"

Jacobi glanced toward the kitchen. "Starving, actually."

"Good. I made grilled lemon rosemary chicken with roasted vegetables and mashed potatoes. Not fancy, but it'll warm you up. And I don't believe in light meals when monsters are on the loose."

Beretti returned, shutting the door behind the dogs. "After dinner, I'm taking us up to the ridge."

Leoni raised a brow. "Another late-night watch party?"

"I've got the drone ready. Thermal's charged. I want a look at the valley tonight."

Leoni asked. "How far can it scan?"

"Couple miles, depending on tree cover."

Leoni gestured toward the hallway. "That's pretty good. Now, go clean up. Both of you."

Jacobi pointed down the hallway. "Shower first?"

Beretti nodded. "Go ahead. I'll check the gear."

As he disappeared down the hall, Beretti grabbed her go-bag and unzipped it on the couch. She pulled out the thermal scope, checked the charge, and made sure the spare drone batteries were loaded into their case. By the time Jacobi returned, steam still rising from his hair, she had everything packed and ready.

"You're up," he said, stepping out in clean clothes.

Beretti took her bag and disappeared down the hall.

Leoni handed Jacobi a glass of water and leaned against the counter. "She still gets that edge in her voice when she's working. I can tell."

Jacobi sipped the water. "She's focused, alright."

"She's also stubborn as hell," Leoni said, not unkindly. "But it's what makes her good."

Leoni watched Jacobi with a faint smile. "She's not always this hard around the edges, you know. Just... here."

Jacobi leaned against the counter, sipping his drink as the sound of running water drifted faintly down the hall. "Yeah. She seems more guarded here. Even more than usual."

Leoni tilted her head thoughtfully. "It's her hometown.

Coming back always pulls something in her tighter."

Jacobi nodded, eyes on the floor. "She carries everything so well, you almost forget she's doing it. But when you try to get closer, ask real questions, it's like she's always holding something just out of reach."

"She wouldn't let you," Leoni said. "She was just a kid when everything flipped. Fourteen, remember? One day she's helping with chores on the farm, the next, she's alone. Ben did what he could, but there's only so much you can carry for someone else. Being a teenager is rough enough, but feeling abandoned, especially the way she sees it, that hits hardest when you're already trying to figure out who you are."

Leoni shook her head. "Not really. She keeps that stuff locked up somewhere she doesn't want to go. Every now and then, if there's enough wine or the right song comes on, she might let something slip. But even then, it's like she's handing you a puzzle piece and hoping you don't ask for the rest."

Jacobi smiled half-heartedly.

"You ever wish she did more than visit once a year?" he asked as he leaned against the table.

"Sometimes," Leoni responded. "But I think she needed to

leave to figure out who she is without this place hanging over her. She always comes back, though. She shows up for Ben. She checks on me. She doesn't really go anywhere else when she visits us so we get all her attention."

Jacobi smiled faintly. "That sounds like her."

Leoni dried her hands and turned to him. "This town isn't just a memory for her. It's layers. There's the part that misses her parents, the part that resents being left behind… and the part that still wishes she could change what happened. I think she felt powerless. She didn't get a chance to say goodbye. And that feeling doesn't go away just because the years do."

Jacobi's voice was quiet. "Whatever's happening out there in those woods, it's stirring more than just old fears. I'll keep an eye on her."

"She'd never ask," Leoni added, "but she'd do the same for you without blinking."

Just then, the water shut off. Footsteps padded softly down the hallway.

Beretti returned, fresh-faced and clean, sleeves rolled. "Let's eat before Ben gets here and finishes the meal on his own."

As if on cue, the front door opened and Ben stepped inside. He looked tired, but steady.

"Hope you saved me a corner," he said, brushing off his coat and setting it on the rack.

Leoni handed him a plate. "Sit. You've got five minutes before I toss the rest to the dogs."

Ben kissed her cheek and slid into his chair. "You're a treasure."

No one said much while they ate.

When the plates were cleared, Beretti and Jacobi stood automatically and began gathering the dishes. Leoni waved them off at first, but Beretti gave her a look that ended the argument.

Jacobi dried while Beretti washed. The rhythm was unspoken but easy. Familiar. Like they'd done it together a dozen times before.

Ben leaned back in his chair, watching them with a faint smile. "You two make a good team."

Beretti glanced over her shoulder. "Don't get used to it. Next time you're drying."

"You won't be able to reach the top shelf," Jacobi said, handing her a dripping glass.

"Keep talking," she said, "and you'll be using paper towels."

Ben chuckled and stood, grabbing his jacket. "So, you wanna head up to the ridge now?"

Beretti nodded. "Yeah. Let's head out. We'll drive slow and set up in the clearing."

Jacobi slung his jacket over his shoulder. "Let's see if the valley's ready to show us something."

Beretti turned to Leoni. "Thanks for dinner. It was perfect."

"Yeah, you're the best, Leoni." Jacobi added as he rubbed a hand over his stomach.

Leoni kissed Ben on the cheek as he passed. "Try not to bring anything home."

He squeezed her hand and gave Wink a quick pat on the head.

The door shut softly behind them, the last of the warm light disappearing as they stepped out into the dark.

CHAPTER 23

The SUV climbed steadily up the narrow ridge road, tires shifting now and then on the uneven, packed dirt. Pines pressed in close, tall and unmoving in the high-beam wash of headlights. Above them, a low ceiling of cloud swallowed the moonlight whole.

Ben shifted in his seat. "Don't forget *Ironhowl Run* kicks off tomorrow night. Hundreds of bikers already came through town, and there'll be more tomorrow."

Jacobi sighed. "Great, more people to deal with."

Ben rubbed his jaw. "We usually just deal with a couple of drunken fights or someone passing out in the wrong spot. But the whole thing's held at the showground that backs right onto the national forest."

He looked at them, concern settling into his features. "That's the part that worries me."

Beretti leaned back slightly. "We'll handle whatever happens as it comes."

They rode the rest of the way in silence until the trees began to thin. The SUV eased onto a shoulder carved into the slope, a wide flat turnout barely visible beneath the branches. Beretti pulled in, turned the wheel, and reversed until the vehicle faced back toward the road.

"Exit plan," she said, cutting the engine.

"I taught you well," Ben said with a smile.

They stepped out into the stillness. The wind didn't move up here. Even the treetops stood quiet, like they were waiting. Beretti unlatched the tailgate and opened her gear case. Jacobi pulled out the thermal binoculars. Ben slung a smaller pack over one shoulder, then moved to the edge of the overlook.

Below them stretched the valley, layered in black and silver. The lights of Blackridge shimmered faintly in the distance, flickering behind ridgelines and hills. Beyond that, the forest took over, unbroken, undisturbed, and vast.

Beretti crouched, locking the drone rotors into place. The LED indicators on the control tablet blinked to life. A soft mechanical whir signaled the drone's readiness.

Ben took in the dark with his bare eyes. "It's a good perch."

"High ground gives the drone more range," Beretti said. "We'll start with a sweep over the eastern line and work west."

The drone rose slowly into the air, lights dim against the night sky. On the tablet, thermal imaging began to feed through, grainy black and white, layered in heat blooms. Jacobi raised his binoculars. Ben took a spare pair and paced slowly across the dirt road.

The first hour passed in shifts of gray and silence. The drone glided above the trees, scanning methodically. They picked up the usual traffic, natural, expected. A pair of coyotes moved along a deer trail, thin and alert, their body heat trailing like ribbons behind them. A herd of deer grazed at the edge of a hollow. A fox darted through brush, then vanished into a narrow den opening. An owl swooped by, wings lit faintly in thermal as it hunted low across the ridge.

Jacobi let out a low breath. "Lot of activity tonight."

Beretti didn't look up from the screen. "All part of the ecosystem."

Ben held steady, binoculars pressed to his eyes. "Watching this is more interesting than most of the garbage on Netflix," he mumbled.

They kept scanning.

Half an hour later, Jacobi lowered the binoculars and rolled his neck.

"Either they are hunting elsewhere tonight or they know we are watching." he said.

"Hard to say," Beretti replied.

Ben finally spoke. "I've seen more happen in this county in the last week than I have in the last two decades. And none of it makes sense."

No one spoke again until Jacobi straightened suddenly, thermal binoculars raised.

"Wait," he said. "I've got something. Mid-tree line, south side. Holding still."

Beretti's eyes flicked to him. "Coordinates?"

He read them off quickly. She adjusted the drone's altitude and swung it around.

The thermal feed flickered, then stabilized.

There, nestled high in the branches of a thick cedar, sat something large.

Its heat signature was faint but clear. Broad shoulders, narrow waist, limbs folded tight against its body. It sat hunched, arms draped over a thick branch, head angled slightly down like it was watching.

"Too big for any local animal," Jacobi said.

Beretti zoomed in.

The shape pulsed subtly with heat, alive and alert. Pointed ears, long limbs. Its stillness felt unnatural. Like a hunter waiting for the signal to pounce.

Ben stepped in behind them. "That looks pretty big."

"It's not a Sasquatch," Jacobi said. "Too lean."

"No," Beretti said. "That's a Dogman."

She adjusted the drone slightly, keeping the camera steady.

Then, on the far edge of the frame, two larger shapes appeared.

Upright. Heavily built. Standing still.

Two Sasquatch.

They were over two hundred yards away, their posture rigid. Not approaching, not retreating. Just holding ground.

Jacobi stared through his binoculars. "Are they watching it?"

"They know it's there," Beretti said. "But they're not rushing in."

Ben spoke low. "Why the hell are they waiting?"

"Because it's waiting too," she replied.

"Well, that answers that. The Sasquatch definitely know something's moved into their territory." Jacobi stated.

Beretti glanced at him but didn't say anything.

For the next twenty minutes, no one moved.

The Dogman stayed in the tree, unmoving. The Sasquatch stood in place, locked in. The entire section of forest below them seemed suspended, caught in the tension of something primal.

Beretti's fingers hovered over the tablet, guiding the drone in a slow, wide circle. The thermal imaging caught every subtle heat bloom, every flicker of motion in the brush that wasn't them.

Then, like a switch flipping, it began.

The Dogman dropped from the tree, limbs flaring as it fell. It hit the ground in a crouch and launched forward in a burst of movement that looked more animal than anything human. Its legs pumped low and fast, arms swaying in sync, every step wild and urgent.

The Sasquatch moved a second later.

One took a wide arc through the trees, flanking with brutal force. The other gave direct chase, thundering through the underbrush on all fours, its head low, and long arms driving it forward in powerful, loping strides.

The drone banked and followed, keeping the chase in frame.

The Dogman cut right, then left, slipping between trees with terrifying ease. It moved on all fours for speed, then surged upright to leap over a fallen log, barely slowing.

The Sasquatch were fast but not as agile. Still, they were relentless. The flanker pushed harder, trying to drive it toward the second. The one behind gained ground in bursts, smashing through brush and snapping low branches as it followed.

"They're closing in," Jacobi said, eyes wide.

Beretti adjusted the altitude. "It's trying to break the perimeter."

Ben grunted. "Not going to make it easy."

The Dogman hit a rocky incline and scrambled up, claws digging into the soil. It reached the top and hesitated for a second. That second nearly cost it. One of the Sasquatch was just behind it.

Instead of continuing straight, the Dogman made a quick turn and leapt onto a thick tree branch that stretched across a narrow ravine. The branch sagged under its weight, but held. It bounded across the limb and pushed off with its hind legs, launching over the ravine in a flash of motion.

It landed hard on the opposite slope, rolled, and vanished into thicker trees.

The Sasquatch stopped at the edge.

One stepped closer to the tree, testing the angle, but it didn't try to follow. The branch wouldn't hold. They stood there, watching before walking away.

Jacobi let out a breath. "Smart bastard."

"Fast and smart," Beretti said. "It knew the terrain."

Ben's voice was quiet. "How those creatures move that fast is beyond me."

Beretti recalled the drone. It returned a few minutes later, whirring softly as it lowered onto the dirt road. She shut it down and packed it carefully.

"We just watched one nearly get caught," Jacobi said. "Now we know for sure."

Beretti nodded. "Yeah. That Dogman got lucky."

Ben looked down into the valley. The trees below held no answers. Only more waiting.

"Ward's going to want to know everything," she said, hefting the gear case.

"Send the footage tonight," Jacobi said. "We might not get another look like that."

They stood there for a few seconds longer.

The woods had gone still again.

No wind.

No sound.

Just silence, unsettling and full of something unseen.

Beretti turned toward the SUV. "Let's get out of here."

They loaded up and drove slowly down the road. The SUV's headlights cut into the dark like spears, leaving the forest to swallow the path behind them.

CHAPTER 24

THE SASQUATCH

The forest hadn't changed. Not really. Not since the young one had drifted away from the clan and never returned.

Even with the body gone, carried off by the hairless ones, the land still held the memory. The shape pressed into the earth.

Blood soaked into the roots. The stink of death. The stink of the other.

The two that stood beneath the trees had not spoken. They didn't need to. What ran through them was older than language. Beneath their silence was a rhythm, a memory that pulsed behind their ribs like a second heartbeat.

One of ours has fallen. The forest calls for balance.

And they had answered.

The one in front crouched near the old cedar, nostrils flaring.

The stink of the creature curled into its senses. It was not new. This was not the first time one of those things had stalked the outer woods. But it had been years.

Generations ago, their kind had known the Dogmen.

Not many. Not often.

But always enough to remember.

Kreth. Sharp teeth on two legs.

The Kreth were not like the hairless ones who came with their noise and metal and fire, or even like the bears that roamed with hunger but not hatred. No. The Kreth were something else. Something wrong.

Sneaky. Evil. Cruel. Vicious.

Not hunters. Not challengers. But destroyers. They came not for need but for pain. They killed without honor, without hunger, without sense.

The Sasquatch did not fear many things.

But they feared letting a Kreth stay.

When they came before, they were run off or crushed. When they left, they left behind ruin.

So when the scent came again, strong and layered over blood and stink, the message was clear.

The creature had not stumbled into their woods.

It had claimed them.

High above, crouched in the crown of a cedar, the Kreth waited.

Its shape radiated wrongness. Long limbs coiled tight. Ears pointed. Shoulders twitching. The Sasquatch saw it even without looking directly. Its heat stained the bark.

They did not stir.

Not yet.

The Kreth was watching.

So were they.

Time passed in silence.

Then the creature moved.

It dropped from the tree, limbs splaying as it fell. It landed without sound, then sprang forward like a shadow cast too far from its source.

The Sasquatch behind followed immediately, feet slamming into the earth. The other moved wide, slipping between trunks, low to the ground, angling to drive the Kreth inward.

The chase had begun.

The Kreth ran like no other thing. It twisted through narrow gaps, bounded over roots, leapt low stones, then dropped to all fours for speed. But it never stopped moving. Never faltered.

It didn't run out of fear.

It ran out of habit.

The Sasquatch were not as fast, but they were tireless. Their breath stayed even. Their stride never broke. They followed with the patience of the mountain, not the speed of the stream.

Closer.

The Kreth shrieked once, harsh and jagged, and pushed

itself harder. It leapt through a fallen arch of old pine, then ricocheted off a low slope, trying to widen the gap.

But the flank tightened. The Sasquatch ahead moved faster, barreling into position, aiming to drive it back toward the other.

A plan formed, wordless and strong.

The Kreth twisted again, slipping into a narrow trench of rock and brush. It climbed the incline, claws biting soil.

At the top, it stopped.

That one second nearly ended it.

The lead Sasquatch came up behind, bursting through brush, arm outstretched to grab the thing by its throat.

Too late.

The Kreth leapt.

Not forward. Up.

It climbed a low-slung tree, then darted along a thick branch that arched across a narrow ravine.

The Sasquatch stopped.

They stepped to the edge of the drop, silent and braced. The branch would not carry their weight. They didn't test it. They knew.

The Kreth reached the middle and looked back.

For a moment, it lingered there, as if proud. As if taunting.

The Sasquatch did not move.

The Kreth turned and leapt again, clearing the ravine in a long, wild arc. It landed in the trees beyond and disappeared.

The woods sank back into silence.

But the stink remained.

The Sasquatch on the left stepped forward, pressed one broad hand to the tree's bark. The branch trembled faintly from the weight it had carried.

That thing had marked their ground.

Killed one of their own.

Marked it with stink.

Left its scent like poison in the leaves.

They would not forget.

They turned without a word and vanished into the forest.

CHAPTER 25

The house was quiet when the trio returned. The porch light was still on, casting a soft glow across the yard. Inside, the dogs didn't bark. They must have recognized the SUV by sound alone. Beretti killed the engine and stepped out, her shoulders stiff from the long day.

Jacobi followed her to the front door, where Ben slid his key in and pushed it open. Warmth and the scent of vanilla soy candle greeted them, along with the soft creak of an old house winding down for the night.

Leoni was curled into one corner of the couch, a well-worn novel in her lap and a blanket around her legs. Whiskey was tucked beside her, snoring gently. Wink perked up when the door opened, his little tail thumping once against the throw rug.

Leoni looked up over the rim of her glasses and smiled.

"Well, look who made it back in one piece. I was about to send the dogs."

Beretti offered a tired grin. "Only if the dogs were armed."

Leoni laughed, rising to her feet and giving Jacobi a light pat on the shoulder. "Next time I'll send them loaded."

Ben stepped out of his boots and set them by the door. "Coffee?"

Beretti shook her head. "Not for me. I've got to call Ward before I crash."

"I'll start a pot anyway," Ben said, already walking toward the kitchen.

Leoni stretched and yawned. "I'm off to bed before I fall asleep sitting up. You boys behave."

She gave Jacobi a small wave and kissed Ben on the cheek before heading down the hallway, dogs trotting close behind.

Jacobi dropped his jacket over the back of a chair as Beretti grabbed her phone out of her pocket.

She stepped outside onto the front porch, lifting the phone to her ear as the door clicked shut behind her.

Ben filled the kettle and lit the stove. Jacobi rubbed the back of his neck, trying to loosen the knot that had formed sometime around the third hour of standing on a ridge staring at trees.

The front door creaked open a few minutes later as Beretti stepped in and leaned against the frame.

"He's not sending anyone," she said. "Wants us to keep documenting and call for backup if we need it. Told me to trust my gut."

Ben poured water into a French press and gave a slow nod. "Sounds like he trusts you both."

"He knows we've got this," she said, her voice low.

"You heading to bed?" Ben asked.

"Yeah." She took a sip of the water she'd left on the counter earlier and headed down the hallway. "Night, boys."

Jacobi watched her go, then glanced back to see Ben collecting two mugs from the shelf.

"Back porch?" Ben asked.

Jacobi nodded. "Sure."

They stepped outside into the cold, each holding a cup of steaming coffee. A few stars had fought their way through the cloud cover. The trees beyond the yard stood dark and motionless.

Jacobi leaned on the rail, mug cradled between both hands.

"She's tough," he said quietly. "Always composed. But tonight... it's like being here presses on something she's been trying not to feel."

Ben didn't speak for a long moment. He blew into his coffee and sat down in the chair closest to the corner of the porch.

"She wasn't always like that," he said finally. "When she was a kid, she had this spark. Always outside. Always chasing something or climbing something she probably shouldn't have."

Jacobi took a seat opposite him, resting his mug on his knee.

"She talk much about her parents?" Ben asked, not looking over.

"Not really. Just that they died when she was fourteen.

Car accident."

Ben gave a faint sound, not quite agreement, not quite anything else.

Ben kept his eyes on the neighbors trees. "Nicole took it hard. As you'd expect. We were down the coast for a few days. She'd been asking to see the ocean, so I figured it was time. While we were there, I got the call. Her parents were gone. I didn't tell her until we were on the way back, but I think she already knew. Something in her shifted. She didn't want to go back to the house. And as far as I know, she hasn't. Not since."

Jacobi's stomach clenched.

"She didn't talk for a while after that," Ben went on. "Weeks, really. Would answer if spoken to, but only just. I tried to keep her close. Moved her in with me. Gave her space when she needed it. She was... empty. Quiet in a way that kids shouldn't be."

Jacobi didn't interrupt.

"When she finally started speaking again, it was to say she didn't believe the accident. She said it didn't feel right. Said her dad was too careful, her mom too attentive. Something didn't add up. She carried that with her. Still does, I think."

Jacobi shifted slightly. "You think she's right?"

Ben met his gaze for the first time. "I think Nicole's got a gut that won't quit. And if her gut tells her something's off, then something probably is."

They sat for a moment, sipping the coffee that had grown slightly bitter with cooling.

"She started hanging with the wrong group a few years later," Ben said. "Local kids, rougher edges. One guy in particular. Twenty-four years old, lived with his cousin out past Old Mill Road. I told her he was no good. She didn't listen."

Jacobi winced. "That happens a lot. Lonely kids trying to fill a void."

Ben nodded. "She went to his place one night. After a party. Friends dropped her off. She was laughing, apparently. Still riding high from the night."

The silence that followed was long and thick.

"He sucker punched her," Ben said. "Right in the temple. Dropped her cold. Wanted to teach her a lesson. Maybe worse."

Jacobi's eyebrows creased.

"She woke up, and by all accounts, didn't scream or cry.

She just got up and beat the hell out of him. Broke his nose. Cracked three ribs. Put him in the hospital."

"Good," Jacobi mumbled.

Ben's eyes didn't change. "She could've gone to jail. I wasn't sheriff back then. Just a mechanic. But I went with her to speak to the authorities. She didn't lie about it. Told them what happened. There were bruises, photos. Friends who testified to her being dropped off. That saved her."

Jacobi looked down at the grain of the wooden deck, tracing it with his eyes.

"She signed up for the military two months later," Ben continued. "Hadn't even finished high school. Got her GED, passed the physicals. She told me she needed to do something that meant something. That if she stayed, she'd drown in the memories."

Jacobi swallowed hard. "Yet, she still carries it."

Ben gave a tired smile. "Every day. It's stitched into her bones. Nicole's not someone who forgets, even when she says she does."

Ben glanced at him then, his brow slightly furrowed. "How long have you two been working together?"

Jacobi sat back. "This is our third job. We were teamed up pretty recently."

Ben nodded. "You seem to work well together."

"We do. She's... solid. Disciplined. I run hot sometimes, and she reins me in without making a scene. She's the voice of reason, every time. I'm the one who charges ahead. She keeps me from doing something dumb. She's more mature than me, no question."

Ben smiled faintly. "She's always been older than her years. Her soul has been here before, no doubt."

He paused, tapping the rim of his mug with a thumbnail.

"You know," Ben added, "the fact that she's stuck with you this long says something. Nicole's never had a one-on-one partner longer than a single assignment. In the early days of Apex Jaegers, Ward tried matching her with a few different agents. Male and female. It never worked out. Personalities clashed, or the rhythm just wasn't right. He kept having to switch them."

Jacobi listened, eyebrows slightly raised.

"Eventually, the team grew bigger. More agents, more flexibility. That's when she found her footing. She blended into the larger group without needing to form those tight pair bonds."

Ben gave him a thoughtful look. "But now, with the team stretched thin, Ward clearly went back to that idea. Paired her up again. And here you are, still standing beside her after three jobs. You've stuck. That means something."

Jacobi chuckled under his breath. "I'll take that as a win."

Ben nodded once. "You should. She must respect you. Probably even enjoys your company, though don't expect her to say it."

Jacobi grinned. "Noted."

Ben leaned back in his chair, the wood creaking. "She doesn't hate this place. Not really. But it reminds her of everything she couldn't change. Everything she lost."

They sat in silence again, letting the steam from their cups drift up into the night air.

Jacobi finally broke it. "How do I help her?"

Ben looked over, face calm, eyes serious. "Don't try to fix her. Just show up. Be steady."

Jacobi nodded slowly.

"She doesn't need sympathy," Ben continued. "She needs truth. She needs someone to tell her she's not broken. That surviving isn't the same as living, and she deserves more than just getting by."

Jacobi drained the last of his coffee and stood, stretching.

"She's lucky to have you."

"No," Ben said. "I'm lucky to have her."

The screen door creaked open and they stepped inside, setting their empty mugs on the counter.

Jacobi turned toward the guest room. "See you in the morning."

Ben nodded once. "Get some rest. Tomorrow's not going to wait."

Jacobi disappeared down the hall.

Ben lingered in the kitchen, one hand on the edge of the counter, staring at nothing.

Then he turned off the light and headed to bed.

CHAPTER 26

The smell of eggs came first, rich, and savory, followed by the scent of something frying in oil, maybe potatoes or sausage. A gentle sizzle rose from the stovetop where Leoni was making breakfast, spatula in one hand and a mug of coffee in the other.

Morning light pressed through the curtains in uneven stripes, catching the steam rising from the pan. The television was on in the corner, one of the local morning shows running on mute, its cheerful hosts gesturing through weather maps and scrolling headlines.

Jacobi leaned against the counter, mug in hand, while Beretti sat at the table with one knee tucked beneath her. She looked relaxed, coffee cup in hand, sleeves pushed to her elbows.

Whiskey lay curled beneath Leoni, and Wink was already

stationed by Jacobi's chair, one eye watching him.

"Ben already left?" Jacobi asked, glancing toward the hallway.

"Quarter past six," Leoni said. "He had to swing by the office early. There was a call about some missing cattle up in the north end, but he said it was probably just a busted fence."

Beretti sipped her coffee. "And if it isn't, we'll hear about it."

Leoni gave a one-shoulder shrug. "You know this place. Things go quiet, people get nervous. Especially this week."

Jacobi took a long drink, savoring the bitter warmth. "I'm surprised there weren't any calls about the Dogman last night. Not even a sighting."

"In some ways, yeah," Beretti said. "But also, those two Sasquatch ran that one Dogman hard out of the area. If that thing has any instincts left, it's licking its wounds somewhere far from here."

Leoni carried the plates over and sat across from Beretti. "I'll take a biker bar fight over that any day."

That made Jacobi lift an eyebrow. "Speaking of which…

what time are we supposed to be at this thing?"

"*The Ironhowl Run*," Leoni said, mouth quirking. "Sounds dramatic, doesn't it?"

Beretti grinned. "Every year. First weekend after the new moon in December. They always start with the evening lineup. Live music, a few food stalls, some local vendors. Tomorrow's the big ride. Hundreds of them, snaking through the hills like chrome ants."

Jacobi raised his mug in a silent toast. "To temporary tinnitus and the smell of burnt rubber."

Leoni laughed. "It's not that bad. Most of the guys and gals are fine. Rowdy but respectful. They come for the food and the music, maybe a tattoo or two. They've only had to break up one serious fight in the past five years. And even that was over who stole someone's nachos."

Beretti chuckled. "Ben still won't let that one go."

"Neither would I," Leoni said, pointing her fork at her. "Food theft is sacred territory."

Jacobi looked between them. "So what exactly is expected of us? Crowd control? Vendor patrol?"

Beretti shrugged. "Sheriff's stretched thin with most of his team split between the town and outlying properties. He just wants extra eyes. Someone around in case anything gets loud or weird. Especially with everything going on."

"Just tonight?" Jacobi asked.

"Tonight for the opening. Tomorrow is the ride but we will just be watching things at the showground until it closes.. After that, they scatter to the wind."

Leoni leaned forward, elbows on the table. "Now the real question. You getting a tattoo while you're there, Jacobi?"

He blinked. "You gotta be joking."

She nodded toward him, playful. "You look like a man who might secretly have something inked where no one can see it. Skull on your ankle? Snake on your lower back?"

Beretti snorted into her coffee.

Jacobi set his mug down, eyes wide with mock offense. "First of all, my lower back is reserved for motivational quotes only. And second, I'd never ruin this temple of a body unless it's what the ladies demand."

Leoni cackled. "Oh, please. I've seen guys bigger than you

cry at the needle."

"It's not the pain I am worried about. It the forever ink on my skin," he said, placing a hand over his chest.

Beretti leaned back in her chair. "You do realize the more you talk, the more this is going to happen, right?"

Jacobi raised an eyebrow. "You're going to get one?"

"I've already got a few."

His eyes lit with curiosity. "Really? Where?"

She just sipped her coffee without answering.

Leoni grinned. "Now you've done it. He is not going to stop wondering where and what."

"I'll survive," Jacobi said. "I'm learning that's the theme around here."

Whiskey let out a sneeze from under the table, and Wink gave a small huff in agreement.

Jacobi sat down with his plate of eggs and grits, and leaned back with a sigh. "Alright. *Ironhowl Run*. I'll wear something that says 'approachable but authoritative.'"

Leoni tilted her head. "Black T-shirt?"

"Exactly."

They shared another laugh before falling into a comfortable quiet.

Outside, the wind picked up. The chime on the porch let out a soft clink. Somewhere in the distance, a motorcycle revved to life.

Jacobi stretched his arms and looked to Beretti. "We rolling in together?"

"Yeah. Let's check in with Ben first. Make sure there's no unexpected chaos before tonight."

Leoni stood and started clearing the plates. "I'll pack you two some snacks. Those vendors are good, but the lines are long and the food's overpriced."

Jacobi stood to help. "You're spoiling us."

"That's because I don't want you coming home cranky," she said, giving him a look. "Hungry agents make bad decisions."

Beretti smiled. "You're not wrong."

They moved around the kitchen in an easy rhythm. Jacobi dried dishes, Beretti wiped down the table, and Leoni stuffed a paper sack with sandwiches, apples, and a few homemade cookies wrapped in wax paper.

As they were getting ready to leave, Wink hopped onto the bench by the door and barked once, abrupt and expectant.

Jacobi bent to scratch behind his ears. "You're the real sheriff of this house, huh?"

"He absolutely is," Leoni said. "Just ask Ben."

Outside, the sun had climbed just enough to warm the windshield. Beretti pulled her jacket on and slung her bag over her shoulder. Jacobi followed her out, tossing the snack bag into the back seat.

The calm before the storm.

Or at least before the engines.

CHAPTER 27

When they pulled up near the southern edge of the event grounds, the *Ironhowl Run* was starting to take shape. Vendors moved in and out of open-sided canopies, adjusting signs, unloading coolers, and rolling out folding tables. The smell of grilling meats hadn't fully taken hold yet, but the promise of it lingered faintly in the afternoon air.

Farther up the gravel path, a converted barn stood with its wide doors open, people moving in and out, hauling in speakers and crates of lighting gear.

Beretti adjusted the strap of her shoulder bag and looked across the field. "Looks like we beat the rush."

"Honestly kind of refreshing," Jacobi said, shutting the SUV door. "Gives us time to check the area before the crazies come out."

They walked into the flow of early foot traffic, moving around clusters of volunteers and vendors. Canopies in bold colors dotted the edge of the clearing, patches, leather vests, bike parts, hot sauces and artisan jerky. The tattoo tent had a few artists setting up their gear, rolls of cord and plastic gloves laid out in tidy rows. Most of the bikers were still arriving, either walking the lot or idling near the barn.

Jacobi pointed to a sign painted in bold red script across one of the barn doors. "Entertainment starts at seven. Guess we've got time to stroll."

Beretti scanned the surroundings. "Let's walk the grounds first. Get the layout, check for any weak spots. If anything stirs tonight, it'll be at the edges."

"Sure," Jacobi said, already surveying the terrain. "Big events like this always feel one spark away from getting complicated."

They passed a row of local vendors, handmade soaps, wood-burned signs, and a guy carving animal skulls into elaborate, haunting designs. A woman selling kettle corn offered them a sample, and Jacobi took a handful with a grateful nod.

"Damn, these are good," he said, tossing a few into his

mouth.

Beretti smiled but bit her tongue.

The barn ahead was the main hub. The sound crew inside tested gear, sending muffled bass lines echoing from the thick walls. Tables and folding chairs were still being set up inside. Strings of lights hung loosely from the rafters, waiting to be powered on. A few staff walked back and forth, taping down cords and testing microphones.

Jacobi tilted his head. "Barn show's a nice touch. Bit of charm with the noise."

Beretti looked around. "And plenty of exits, which makes it easier if things go south."

They kept walking, passing a group of bikers leaned against a row of bikes. One of them recognized Beretti and tipped his chin in greeting. She returned it with a smile but didn't stop.

"So far, so good," Jacobi said, looking over his shoulder. "Crowd's thin. Everyone's still in setup mode."

"It won't stay that way for long," she replied. "By six, this field's going to be packed."

They turned off the main path and followed a trail that ran parallel to the fencing. The woods pushed closer here, and the din of the event dulled beneath the canopy. Behind them, a generator buzzed to life, followed by the distant rumble of another bike pulling into the gravel lot.

"This would be the weak spot," Beretti said, motioning toward a section of loose mesh fencing. "If something came through here, no one inside would see it until it was too late."

Jacobi ran a hand along one of the metal stakes. "We'll want a patrol swing past this area once the crowd thickens. Quiet paths make good cover."

They circled back around the barn from the far side, passing the food trucks now lining up along the outer loop. A few were already cooking. Smoke curled from the top of a trailer labeled RIB KING, and the smell of charred meat floated into the breeze.

Jacobi let out a long sigh. "You know what? I take back every joke I made. This smells incredible."

"Ironhowl's never skimped on the food," Beretti said. "Ben says it's the only reason half the town tolerates the noise."

As they rounded back toward the vendor tents, they passed a small open booth with three people setting up a pop-up tattoo station. One of them, a tall guy with a shaved head and sleeves of ink, glanced at Jacobi and pointed at his arm.

"You look like a man in need of a bad decision."

Jacobi smirked. "Tempting, but I can make bad decisions without the pain."

"Your loss," the artist said with a wink, going back to sorting needles.

Leoni's teasing from that morning flashed in Jacobi's head, and he chuckled to himself.

"You really don't have any ink?" Beretti asked, glancing over.

"Nope."

She raised an eyebrow. "Not even college regret?"

"I'm from L.A.," he said. "Our version of rebellion was sleeping through yoga class and forgetting to recycle."

Beretti gave him a sideways smile but said nothing.

They passed a security tent with two volunteers sitting at a folding table. Both smiled as they approached.

"Any issues?" Beretti asked.

"Not yet," one of them replied. "It's mostly just prep right now. Everything should kick off in the next couple hours."

Jacobi looked toward the barn, now glowing slightly from the lighting tests inside. "Let's keep an eye on how many come through after dark. That'll be when things start to get loose."

They finished their loop, ending back near the SUV. The crowd was building now, but slowly. There was still time before the noise hit its peak.

Beretti looked across the clearing. "We'll stay close tonight. Rotate sides every half hour or so. Just enough visibility to make a presence known."

"Sounds good," Jacobi said. "Let's keep it uneventful."

They watched as another rider pulled in, engine growling, headlights cutting across the lot.

The Ironhowl was just getting started.

CHAPTER 28

The barn throbbed with sound and light. Guitars wailed over a pounding beat, the crowd inside surging like a tide to the rhythm of the music. Outside, floodlights, and strings of bulbs cast a hazy glow across the lot, catching on beer bottles, leather vests and the silver zippers of denim jackets. Smoke curled from the grill lines, and the air carried that winter-stung blend of hot food, engine oil, cold breath and wood dust.

Beretti leaned against the barn wall near the open doors, arms crossed. She watched the crowd with a quiet stillness. Hundreds of people danced or drank or leaned in close to speak over the sound. It was loud, raucous, messy in that way festivals always were.

Ben stood focused on the crowd, talking to one of his deputies.

Jacobi was sipping a cup of something sweet from one of the stands. "Place is packed now," he said. "Must've doubled since we walked it."

Beretti answered, eyes still scanning. "This is when the trouble usually starts."

Jacobi tilted his cup. "Speaking of which... do you know her?"

He angled his head subtly toward a woman standing across the barn entrance with three others. The woman had dark eyes, eighties-styled auburn hair, a deep cut tank top with silver chains layered across her chest, and a body language that screamed aggression. She was staring hard at Beretti.

Beretti's expression dropped immediately. "Yeah," she said. "That's Tania. Went to high school with her."

"She's been staring at you for ten minutes."

"I noticed."

Jacobi watched her for a beat, then turned his attention back to the crowd. "Friend?"

"Old friend. Until she wasn't."

The music inside picked up tempo, bass thudding deep into the floorboards. Laughter and shouts rippled across the lot as someone near the beer stand tried to climb onto a cooler and failed spectacularly.

Beretti rolled her eyes. Jacobi chuckled.

A sound broke through the crowd. Piercing, high, and ragged. A scream. It cut through the parking lot like a blade, rising from the direction of the bikes.

People froze. Heads snapped toward the noise. Conversations dropped.

A second scream came, even higher, more panicked than the first.

Jacobi was already moving.

Beretti took off right behind him, sidearm still holstered but ready.

Ben turned to his deputies. "Lock this place down. Keep everyone here."

And then he ran.

The noise of the barn faded behind them as the three of them sprinted toward the sound. Past the vendor tents and the food trucks.

Toward the dark.

Toward the scream.

CHAPTER 29

They ran hard, boots pounding the dirt, hearts drumming faster than their feet. The barn's glow disappeared behind them as the sound of the scream guided them like a beacon.

The parking area loomed ahead, rows of bikes lined up like chrome bones under the festival lights. Some still gleamed, freshly polished, others dulled by road grime. People had spilled toward the area by now, drawn by the noise, standing at a distance and whispering.

Jacobi reached the woman first.

She was on her knees, hands pressed to her mouth, sobbing so hard it shook her body. One hand was smeared with blood. Her other trembled as she pointed between two Harleys.

Beretti and Ben arrived just behind him.

Between the bikes lay a body.

No, not just a body. A statement.

The man's torso had been shoved between the machines, bent and twisted, legs splayed at awkward angles. One arm was gone from the elbow down, ragged bone jutting from the torn flesh. His shirt was soaked with blood, ripped open, and across his abdomen were deep, cruel slashes, wide and vicious. His neck was twisted, nearly severed, and his face was frozen in an expression of pure terror.

Beretti crouched, eyes scanning the scene. Blood was everywhere. Spray on the asphalt. Thick drops leading from the rear lot. A trail. She followed it with her eyes and saw where it disappeared into the shadows beyond the lights. The brush.

Jacobi knelt beside the woman, voice low. "Hey. Hey, you're okay. What's your name?"

The woman tried to answer, but no words came. Just a choked sob and a nod toward the body.

Beretti stood. "Ben. We need this area cordoned off. Now."

Ben didn't hesitate. He turned, grabbed his radio, and started issuing orders. Within minutes, deputies were fanning out, pushing people back, unspooling yellow tape. A deputy moved to block the view with a sheriff's SUV, lights pulsing but silent.

An ambulance pulled in fast, tires skidding slightly as it came to a stop. Paramedics jumped out and moved to the woman. She didn't resist as they lifted her gently, whispering to her, wrapping a blanket around her shoulders. One of them glanced at the body and blanched.

Beretti stepped aside as they loaded the woman into the rig.

Jacobi stood beside her, eyes scanning the lot.

"This wasn't a kill. This was a display."

Beretti nodded. "The way he's posed. The positioning. It wanted someone to find him."

Ben joined them, face grim. "He local?"

Jacobi shook his head. "One of the bikers. We saw him earlier. Had a snake tattoo on his scalp."

Ben sighed. "No one saw it happen?"

"Not yet," Beretti said. "But it came from the brush. Trail's fresh. You can smell it."

Beretti crouched again, examining the wounds. "The cuts are deep. These weren't meant to kill fast."

Ben's voice dropped. "It's sending a message."

"To us," Jacobi said.

Beretti stood. "Or to the Sasquatch. Or both."

A deputy walked over. "We're clear past the perimeter. No more people coming through. You want us to start a canvas?"

Ben nodded. "Check the other side of the lot. Behind the vendor trucks too. Talk to everyone. Someone must've heard something. Oh, and keep your firearm handy."

As the deputy left, Beretti turned to Jacobi. "Get photos. I'll document the blood trail. Before the coroner moves anything."

Jacobi already had his phone out. He crouched again, snapping shots from every angle. The flash lit the man's face in stark, ugly bursts.

Beretti moved toward the shadowed edge of the parking lot, tracing the blood trail. It curved behind a trailer, dipped near a line of trash cans, then disappeared into a narrow path between trees.

"Ben walked beside her, careful not to step on any tracks. His hand hovered near his sidearm, eyes sweeping the path ahead."

The trail stopped abruptly near a patch of torn earth.

There were footprints, massive and deeply pressed into the soil, bipedal with long, curved claws. A clear path in and out, as if it had come, killed, and vanished like smoke.

Beretti stood still for a long second, breathing through her nose, tasting the air.

It was still there. That stink of rot and wet fur. The signature scent of something unnatural.

Ben didn't say a word, just stared at the size of the prints with disbelief.

She turned to him. "It watched them. Maybe watched the whole crowd."

Ben glanced at her. "And waited for the right moment."

They headed back toward Jacobi.

He looked up from his phone as they approached. "This is the worst one yet."

"I know," Beretti said.

Ben looked between them. "So what now?"

Beretti replied, "We hold the perimeter tonight. No one goes into the woods until daylight."

Ben gave a slow nod. "Agreed. Last thing I need is a deputy going missing."

Jacobi rubbed at his jaw. "We sweep at first light."

"We'll walk it ourselves if we have to," Beretti said. "But not in the dark."

Ben checked his phone again. "Coroner's about thirty minutes out."

Laughter from the barn drifted faintly toward them. A band had started playing again, but the music felt disconnected, wrong somehow.

"I'll call in everyone," Ben said. "You two stay close tonight. Eyes open. If it shows again…"

"We'll be ready," Beretti said.

CHAPTER 30

The morning air clung cold over the *Ironhowl Run* parking lot, clear and biting against the skin. Gray light sifted through low clouds, casting everything in a pale, unfinished wash.

Beretti stepped out of the SUV and zipped her jacket. The smell of fuel hung in the air, mixed faintly now with blood and something more primal. She glanced around the lot. Four deputies stood at different posts, eyes sweeping the perimeter like silent watchmen.

Ben approached from the far end, one hand resting on his shotgun. "Locals are still waking up. Most of the out-of-towners think last night was a freak incident. We've kept the details tight. There's less foot traffic today now that the run's officially started, but the vendors are still open for the locals and any tourists drifting through."

Beretti nodded. "Fewer people the better."

He motioned toward a deputy standing near the rear cruiser. "That's Deputy Ellis. He'll be joining us. I don't like going in light."

Ellis was young, maybe mid twenties, but there was steel in his stance. His rifle was slung neatly across his chest, and he nodded respectfully. "Morning, Agents."

Beretti returned the nod. "Stay alert. Let's move."

They crossed the edge of the parking lot and stepped into the treeline.

The moment they entered the woods, the world shifted. Sound seemed to stop. The trees closed in, tall and dark, and the undergrowth clung wet to their boots. Pine needles muffled their footsteps, and a dense stillness surrounded them from every angle.

Beretti crouched at the spot where the creature had vanished the night before. "Here. This is where it walked back into the woods."

She brushed the loose earth aside, revealing broad footprints sunk deep into the soil. Each toe ended in a curved claw, etched into the ground as if the creature wanted them noticed.

Jacobi stood behind her, scanning the trail. "This thing didn't rush."

Ben adjusted his grip on the shotgun. "It knew we'd follow."

Ellis didn't speak, but his eyes stayed sweeping the trees.

They followed the trail slowly, moving deeper into the forest. Ten minutes in, Jacobi pointed to a tree trunk on the right. "There."

Five deep claw marks sliced down the bark, clean and fresh. They started at least seven feet up.

Beretti approached and touched the grooves. "Still splintered. Done last night."

Jacobi moved to a lower branch where something had snagged. "Fur," he said, pulling a tangle free.

Beretti took it from him and held it between her fingers. "Almost like bear fur. But too wiry."

Ben sniffed the air and grimaced. "Still stinks."

They pressed on, the terrain rising slightly beneath their feet. The footprints continued, bipedal, heavy, widely spaced.

At one point, they noticed a change in the pattern.

"It circled here," Beretti said, standing still. "You can see the way it turned in place."

Jacobi studied the path ahead. "Was it stalking something? Or just making sure we'd pick up the trail?"

Ben scanned the canopy. "It wanted us to find this."

Eventually, they reached a large outcrop of rock. The prints led up to it, then vanished. No more markings on the other side. No crushed foliage. No sign of descent.

Jacobi looked to the trees above. "There. Broken branch."

Beretti followed his gaze. "Fifteen feet up."

Ellis let out a breath. "That's not natural."

Beretti crouched near the edge and touched the stone. "It climbed. Or jumped. Either way, it's gone from here."

Ben frowned, eyes on the surrounding brush. "You think it's still nearby?"

Beretti stood and looked back toward the trail they'd followed. "Given how quiet it is here, I'd say it is watching.'

Beretti turned to him. "Mark this spot. Send me the coordinates. We're not going farther today."

Jacobi nodded and pulled out his phone.

Ben scanned the woods a final time.

Beretti took one last look at the broken branch above the outcrop. "It waited for the right moment. Slipped out while the crowd was distracted, made the kill, then vanished again without fear."

Jacobi checked the GPS pin. "That confidence worries me more than the claws."

"It should," Beretti said. "Because it hasn't left."

Jacobi paused and looked over his shoulder.

"I definitely feel like we are being watched. Or is it just me?"

Beretti didn't say anything for a second. "No. Not just you."

Ben grunted quietly. "Let's get moving."

They didn't run.

But they didn't waste any time either.

CHAPTER 31

By the time Beretti, Jacobi, Ben and Ellis had returned to the parking lot at Ironhowl Run, the air had shifted.

Not just the cold or the wind, but something else. Pressure. Heat without temperature.

Raised voices echoed across the lot.

A cluster of bikers had gathered near the caution tape, shoulder to shoulder, fists clenched at their sides. Leather, denim, steel chain loops. Faces flushed with grief, frustration and suspicion. A crowd that didn't need much to catch fire.

"Somebody murdered Darryl!" one of them shouted. He was broad and graying, face red with anger. "You just gonna stand around while someone walks away from this? While one of us gets butchered and dumped like roadkill?"

The deputies standing near the tape didn't respond right

away. One tried to raise a hand in a calming gesture, but it wasn't working.

Jacobi looked over at Beretti. "Here we go."

Ben stepped forward, shoulders squared but calm, and walked directly into the middle of the rising tension.

A younger man nearby spoke up. "We were supposed to ride out at dawn. Darryl's crew said they wouldn't go without him. Nobody wanted to leave him behind. So we stayed."

Beretti kept her face neutral, but she understood. They weren't just riders. They were family. And one of their own had been left in pieces.

Ben raised his voice just enough to cut through the noise. "We're doing everything we can. But if you want answers, I need you to let us do our job. Right now that means staying back and keeping calm."

The crowd didn't like it. But they listened. At least for now.

The man who'd been yelling turned to him. "You the one in charge?"

"I'm the sheriff," Ben said.

"Then maybe you can explain what the hell's going on. You got a body ripped open and dumped between two bikes, and you're telling us nothing?"

Ben didn't flinch. "First off, no one was murdered."

That earned a round of mumbled protests and disbelief.

Ben held up a hand. "Let me finish. What happened to Darryl wasn't done by a person. This wasn't a stabbing. It wasn't a shooting. There's no killer in the crowd."

The man narrowed his eyes. "Then what are you saying?"

"I'm saying it was a wild animal," Ben replied, voice steady. "A predator. Big enough and strong enough to do damage before anyone knew it was there."

Another biker near the back scoffed. "Bull. You trying to cover your ass?"

"We're not covering anything," Ben said. "We're looking at prints, markings, injuries. I won't go into detail, but I've seen enough in this job to know what I'm looking at. This wasn't some back-alley fight. It was an attack. Quick. Violent. And not human."

The crowd shifted. Some murmured among themselves,

uncertain now. Others still looked ready to argue.

Beretti stepped forward just enough to be seen but not to overtake the moment. "We know how it sounds. We also know how it looks. But if we thought someone was walking around killing people, we'd say so."

Jacobi joined her. "And if that were the case, we wouldn't be here talking. We'd be hunting a suspect."

The man who'd first shouted stepped back slightly, folding his arms. "So what now? We're supposed to just go back to the rally like nothing happened?"

Ben looked at the group. "Do you want us to shut it down? Cancel the rest of the weekend?"

A few voices responded immediately.

"No way."

"We didn't ride here just to turn around."

"No need for that."

Ben nodded. "Then we move forward with caution. Stick to the main venue. Stay in groups after dark. You see something strange, report it. Don't go looking to handle it yourselves."

A younger man with a spider tattoo on his neck mumbled, "You gonna keep the perimeter locked down?"

"We'll have deputies on rotation throughout the night," Ben replied. "No one's alone out here. Not you, not us."

Another man spoke up, quieter this time. "And what if that thing comes back?"

Ben's voice lowered slightly. "Then we'll be ready for it."

There was a pause. Not agreement, but something close. A cooling. The crowd's edges began to loosen. Some of the bikers turned, mumbling to each other, a few walking off toward their bikes. Others lingered, still watching with wary eyes, not quite convinced but not as close to boiling over.

The man with the beard gave Ben a hard look. "If something else happens, Sheriff, it's on you."

Ben met his gaze without blinking. "Then I guess I'd better make sure nothing does."

As the group dispersed gradually, Jacobi exhaled, long and quiet. "Well that could've gone sideways."

"It still might," Beretti said, watching the treeline.

CHAPTER 32

THE DOGMAN

It had been sleeping. Coiled beneath root and moss, limbs tucked beneath its thick body, hidden in the place where light never fully touched. The air was damp, rich with soil and rot. Its mind had drifted in fragments, images of dark rivers, bones in water, a long ago chase beneath moonlight. But the noise had returned.

Vibrations first. Then the snarling sounds that rolled like thunder through the trees.

It opened its eyes.

The noise came in waves, breaking the quiet apart. Not the calls of prey or the low voices of the hairless ones gathering. These were louder. Not natural. A chorus of growls, rising and falling with no breath between.

It shifted its weight and crept to the edge of its shelter.

Below the ridge, the path cut through the forest like an ugly wound, stripped of stone and softened earth. Shapes moved fast along it, many of them. The scent rose thick and clinging. Not bark, not blood, not fur. Sour. Dry. Tainted. It recoiled from it.

It waited.

Most of them passed quickly, one after another. It watched, low to the ground, only the yellow gleam of its eyes visible beneath the ferns. The group moved as one, loud and clumsy, not worth following. The smell of their movement burned its nose.

Then one broke off.

A single growl faded toward the bend and slowed. The noise stuttered and fell silent.

It rose slowly.

From the trees, it saw the figure swing a leg down and dismount the machine. Female. She lifted the metal covering from her head, then bent down, her hands busy near the machine's belly, softly cursing. The sound meant nothing, but her voice carried the weight of frustration.

She was alone.

It moved downhill through the brush, slipping between roots and fern with ease. Each step was slow and precise. The forest swallowed its sound. It had hunted this way before. Let others pass, waited for the one who strayed.

She straightened again, stepped back from the machine, and reached for something in her jacket. Her scent reached it, skin, sweat, faint sweetness beneath.

It came closer.

She looked down at the small glowing object in her hand, tapping it, mumbling. Her eyes flicked up the trail, scanning behind her. Still no others.

She turned to step off the path and into the grass.

It moved in.

She heard something this time. Froze. Looked back, not quite in the right direction.

It stopped.

She crouched again, searching for whatever she had dropped.

The moment snapped.

It broke from the trees and crossed the distance in four powerful strides.

She looked up too late.

Its arms caught her from behind. One around her chest, the other dragging her back by the hair.

She screamed, once, and clawed at its arm.

It dragged her into the brush.

She thrashed. Elbows struck. Fingers tore at its skin. It welcomed it. The fight tasted sweeter than quietness. She kicked at its legs, dug her nails in, twisted her body sideways to break free.

It didn't slow.

She screamed again, but the sound was short, cut off as her head struck the trunk of a fallen tree. The breath went out of her. Her limbs flailed again, less certain.

It gripped her jaw with one hand and slammed her head against the bark.

The bone cracked.

She went limp.

It tore into her with a frenzy. Claws sank through the meat of her side, tore across her ribs. Her spine arched. Her mouth opened again, no sound this time, just breath, and blood. Her eyes rolled wide.

It bit into her throat and ripped free.

Warm spray hit the leaves. Her legs kicked once more, then stilled.

It crouched over her, breathing fast now, chest rising and falling with each shudder.

The machine still sat above on the path, lights blinking dimly.

It grabbed her by the arms and dragged her into the trees, down toward the hollow. The forest took her blood into its roots. Leaves clung to her face. Her boots caught on stones and snapped branches as her body was pulled deeper.

It found the flat space where the ground dipped into rock. Dropped her there.

Stared at her.

Watched for movement.

None came.

It licked the blood from its forearm and stood.

Far off, another machine rumbled closer. A slow one. Alone.

It vanished into the brush before the noise crested the hill.

Minutes later, another figure arrived.

He called out once. Looked around. Stepped off his machine and spotted the helmet in the ditch.

Picked it up.

He searched the trees.

She was gone.

There was no sound. No sign of the one who had taken her.

CHAPTER 33

Bikers lingered at the edge of the woods. Some stood silent, staring into the trees. Others paced or argued quietly with deputies, asking questions no one could answer.

The woman's bike sat where she'd left it, engine off, helmet in the ditch beside it. A single boot rested a few feet away, half buried in torn grass.

Beretti ducked under the tape and moved in, Jacobi close behind.

One of the deputies gestured toward the ditch. "Guy following a minute or so behind her said she pulled off here. He found the helmet. Called it in right after."

Beretti crouched, examining the ground. There was blood, soaked into the soil and smeared in arcs through the flattened brush.

"Looks like she was dragged," Jacobi said. "Pretty violently too."

They followed the trail into the trees. The path of destruction was clear. Broken branches, streaks of red, deep scuffs in the dirt where her body had been dragged. Near the trunk of a downed tree, they found more blood. A lot more.

Beretti stopped.

"This is where it ended," she said.

The dirt was dark and wet. Spattered leaves clung to the underbrush, some still trembling from the wind or something that had passed too recently.

Jacobi stepped around her, scanning the perimeter. "Kill site."

He pointed to the bark. "Head trauma. Blunt force. Probably threw her against it."

Beretti didn't respond right away. Her eyes followed the line of broken ferns that continued beyond the clearing, winding down a narrow, rocky slope.

The terrain changed sharply just ahead. Jagged stone jutted from the forest floor. The brush thickened, snarled in vines and shadows. A drop-off waited just beyond.

Jacobi climbed a few steps down, then stopped. "We're not getting through that. Not safely."

"No," Beretti agreed. "Too steep. Too easy to get lost."

He came back up and stood beside her.

Behind them, voices drifted faintly from the road. The tension in the air hadn't lifted. A few bikers were still asking what had happened and where she'd gone. The deputies were holding them back, but it wouldn't last forever.

Beretti turned her attention to the blood-soaked leaves again.

"She gave it her best fight," she said. "That much is clear."

Jacobi kept his gaze on the slope. "It probably waited for one to break from the pack and when she did, it took the opportunity. Ambushed her and dragged her in here before anyone came by."

Beretti said solemnly. "The moment she stopped, she was as good as dead."

"Yeah. What terrible luck," Jacobi added.

They walked back through the trail, careful not to disturb the signs. As they broke through the brush and stepped back into view, a few of the bikers leaned forward. One woman looked like she'd been crying. Another man paced in small loops, mumbling to himself.

Beretti walked over to the nearest deputy and spoke softly. "Keep them back. No speculation. No confirmation. Not yet. We will call in a specialist team better skilled and equipped to manage that terrain. Hopefully they can find her remains."

The deputy nodded and moved to intercept a pair of men trying to look past the tape.

Beretti looked at the blood on her boots, then back toward the road.

Some of the Dogmen hunted in packs. Others roamed alone. That unpredictability made tracking them nearly impossible, and Beretti knew it.

CHAPTER 34

The house was still when the pair returned. Late afternoon light filtered in as Whiskey lifted her head, tail thumping once before she curled back beside Wink, who didn't bother moving at all.

Leoni had left a lasagne in the oven and a note on the counter that simply read: Eat. Sleep. Breathe.

They did all three.

One by one, they took showers, letting the steam chase the chill from their bones. The meal was eaten without much talking. They were worn thin, and the quiet felt more like preservation than awkwardness. Beretti stretched out on the couch with a blanket over her legs, eyes half-closed. Jacobi sank into the armchair, a half-empty cup of coffee balanced on the armrest.

It wasn't deep sleep, not for either of them, but it was enough to take the edge off.

By the time they returned to the rally grounds just after seven, the crowds had thinned considerably. Vendors had shuttered their booths at dusk, and the last few food trucks were packing up. The barn still thumped with low music, its lights glowing faintly across the lot.

Beretti adjusted the collar of her jacket and glanced at Jacobi. "Weirdly calm."

Jacobi scanned the grounds. "Yeah, I don't trust it."

They started a perimeter sweep together, taking their time near the vendor rows and back pathways. A few people still milled about near the barn entrance, laughing and swaying with drinks in hand. The rally's energy had quieted, but hadn't vanished.

CHAPTER 35

Beretti walked alongside Jacobi, a paper cup warming her hands. Her coffee had gone lukewarm, but she drank it anyway. The air had turned colder since sunset, biting at the edges of her collar.

A group of kids tore past them, shouting something about racing to the barn. One of them clipped her arm as he ran by. The cup tilted, and the rest of her coffee splashed across her sleeve and chest.

She stopped, blinking.

"Seriously?" she mumbled, holding her arm out.

Jacobi turned. "You good?"

Beretti flicked coffee from her hand. "Yeah. Just soaked and now smell like hazelnut."

The kid kept running, completely unaware.

Jacobi smiled. "That's the second time tonight someone's nearly bowled you over."

Beretti gave him a look and rolled her eyes. "I'll be right back. Gonna clean this up before it dries."

"Want me to walk you over?"

"Thanks, but I think I can handle a bathroom on my own."

He raised a hand in surrender. "I'll grab another round of coffee."

She turned toward the restroom building near the corner of the lot, weaving past a few smokers and a girl in glitter-streaked face paint trying to light a cigarette without success.

Inside, the washroom was quiet, lit by pale overhead bulbs that gave the space a washed-out look. Beretti stood hunched over the sink, hands wet and sticky with coffee. The splash had hit her chest and run down her arm.

She turned the water off and reached for the paper towel dispenser, pulling several sheets. She wiped her forearm first, then dabbed at the damp patch on her shirt before scrubbing roughly at her hands. The sound echoed in the empty room.

The door behind her opened.

Beretti stiffened, looking up at the reflection in the mirror.

Tania.

Of course it was Tania.

She stepped inside like she owned the place, clutching a drink that was mostly ice and whatever sweet red mix passed for alcohol around here. Her makeup looked slept-in, and her hair was pulled up in a way that said she hadn't tried too hard. Scuffed boots, torn leggings, and a ripped tank top under an old jacket completed the look.

Beretti drew in a slow breath and looked back down at the sink. "Not now."

Tania leaned against the tiled wall, one boot dragging a mark on the floor as she cocked her head like a crow waiting for something to fall. Her voice had that familiar rasp to it, half-smoke, half-bite. "Don't wanna face the music, huh?"

Beretti didn't answer. She tossed the paper towel into the bin and ran more water, focusing on the lines of her fingers, the tiny cut on her wrist, anything but the woman watching her like a snake waiting for a twitch.

Tania smirked, lifting her cup. "Did you know Quinn died?"

That stopped her.

Beretti's spine went rigid, but she didn't turn.

Tania let the words hang, lazy and mean. "It was six years ago. Motorcycle accident. He hit a patch of gravel out on 89, laid the bike down hard. Didn't even make it to the hospital. Died right there in the dirt."

Beretti reached for another towel. Her face stayed calm, but her eyes were sharp.

"You hear me?" Tania barked, louder now.

"I heard you."

"Guess you were too busy saving the world to check in."

Beretti crumbled the towel and dropped it in the trash. "I don't have time for your crap."

Tania's eyes gleamed. She took a long sip, ice clinking as she chewed on a piece. "You always thought you were better than the rest of us. Like this town was something you needed to scrape off your boots. We used to be tight, remember? Then you put my cousin in the hospital. My *cousin*. And just vanished."

Beretti turned, arms folded, jaw set.

Tania smiled wider. "Bet you haven't even gone back to the old house."

A flicker. Just a moment. But it was enough.

"I didn't think so," Tania said, voice sweet as rot. "And I bet you haven't talked to ole man Richards either."

Beretti narrowed her eyes. "Why would I talk to him?"

That was the crack Tania had been digging for. She grinned wide, stepping close enough that her breath smelled like fruit punch, vodka and stale cigarettes.

"To find out the truth, bitch."

The last word was whispered like a dare. Then Tania spun on her heel and walked out, slow and satisfied, her boots scuffing the tiled floor.

The door swung shut behind her.

Beretti stood alone in the bathroom, the air now feeling

colder than it had before. The sink continued to drip. One slow beat at a time.

She stared at her reflection.

Not at her face.

Not at her eyes.

But at something deeper.

Something shifting.

Behind her, the faint sounds of the rally drifted through the walls, music, muffled laughter, the thump of feet on the barn floor.

But inside the washroom, there was only silence.

And the chill of a name she hadn't thought about in years.

Quinn.

And ole man Richards.

And the house she hadn't stepped inside since the day before her parents died.

Beretti grabbed her jacket from the hook, pulled it on, and walked out the door without looking back.

CHAPTER 36

The last of the vendor trucks rumbled off the gravel lot, brake lights flickering through the trees before disappearing into the dark. One by one, the empty stalls went quiet. Folding tables stacked, coolers dragged away, lights snapped off.

The rally was winding down. Just a few stubborn bikers lingered near the barn, finishing beers and conversations they probably wouldn't remember in the morning. Deputies would be having a field day pulling some of them over for DUIs before the night was out.

Beretti leaned against the fence near the gate, arms crossed. Jacobi stood beside her, hands in his jacket pockets.

"Can't believe we're still standing after the past couple of days," he said.

Beretti looked back toward the barn. "At least it's nearly

done."

Jacobi gave a soft grunt. "Small victories."

They waited until the last taillight vanished down the road. Jacobi pulled the gate closed behind them and latched it. Beretti checked the lock twice before turning back toward their SUV.

"You tired?" Jacobi asked.

She shook her head. "Not even close."

"Me neither."

They stopped by a gas station just outside the town limits. A dim overhead light buzzed softly as Beretti emerged with two steaming coffees. She handed one to Jacobi through the open passenger door.

"Can't promise it's not jet fuel," she said.

Jacobi chuckled. "Even better."

The SUV climbed steadily into the outskirts of Blackridge, weaving through familiar backroads. They turned off onto a narrow dirt pull-off Beretti knew well, one that looped around a wide clearing where hunters and hikers sometimes parked. She reversed in, the SUV facing the exit.

The spot was boxed in on three sides by thick forest. Before them, a peaceful field glowed softly under the moonlight.

"This overlook feeds into a major game trail," Beretti said. "Elk, deer, everything funnels through here eventually."

Jacobi looked through the windshield at the open stretch. "I see. Good spot if something's passing through. Dogmen included."

She turned off all lights.

The moon was out and high. Pale and flat behind the cloud layers, but enough to see by. They left the windows cracked slightly, the air cool but still.

Time passed in silence.

Occasional rustling. Wind slipping through the trees. Somewhere far off, an owl hooted once, then nothing.

The caffeine took the edge off the weariness but not the tension.

Jacobi shifted in his seat and glanced her way. "Can I ask you something?"

Beretti kept her eyes on the treeline. "You can try."

"What did your parents look like?" he asked. "Only if you're willing to talk about it."

She was quiet for a beat, then said softly. "It's fine."

Jacobi waited, patient.

"I'm a mix of the two," she said. "The blonde hair came from my mother's father. He was Swiss. Everyone else on both sides had dark hair. There's a funny story about how my grandmother, who was Native, met him. I'll have to tell you sometime."

She leaned back slightly, arms crossed. "My mother was beautiful. Long straight hair. I always wished I had gotten her hair when I was growing up. Still do, actually. Strong jaw, almond-shaped brown eyes. She was quiet around strangers but lit up with family. Dad…" She exhaled softly. "He looked a lot like Ben. Same smile, same voice. But he was taller. Bit more lean. Carried himself different. Always alert, like he couldn't turn it off."

Jacobi smiled, his gaze fixed ahead. "I can picture them."

Silence settled again, but this time it didn't feel as heavy.

Somewhere in the dark, a twig cracked. Both of them turned toward the sound, eyes scanning the edge of the clearing.

Jacobi stretched out his legs. "You ever think about having a simpler life?"

Beretti looked over at him. "Define simpler."

He shrugged. "You know. Family. Kids. A nine-to-five. Maybe a dog, a normal mortgage. The kind of life that doesn't involve forest stakeouts and monsters."

She snorted. "Getting personal now, are we?"

"We're sitting in a car staring at a moonlit field. Feels like the time."

Beretti looked ahead for a moment, then said, "Sometimes the idea sneaks in. A little version of life that makes sense. But a bigger part of me knows I wouldn't last long. I'd go nuts without some sort of chaos. Normal isn't... normal for me."

Jacobi smiled faintly. "That's what teenagers are for. They create chaos just fine."

They both laughed.

Then Beretti asked, "What about you?"

He grew quiet for a second. "Yeah, I've thought about it. Daydreamed. But I don't think I'd make a good dad."

"Why's that?"

"My old man wasn't. Guess I don't know what good looks like."

Beretti was about to answer when a foul smell drifted in through the cracked windows.

She blinked. "Tell me that wasn't you."

Jacobi sniffed, then shook his head and lifted his arm to cover his face. "Nope. Not me."

Another minute passed.

A faint tapping sound came from the roof. Something small.

Beretti leaned forward and looked up. "Did something just hit us?"

Jacobi nodded, squinting upward. "Sounded like a pebble."

Another followed. Then another. Soft taps, like something testing them.

They kept coming, more regular now. Gradually increasing in size.

Jacobi shifted in his seat. "Pretty sure we're not alone."

Beretti sighed. "You've got to be kidding me."

Beretti scanned the field, the tree line. Nothing moved. But the smell was stronger now. Pungent. Musky. Almost overwhelming.

"I don't see anything," she said.

"Neither do I. But it's close."

Beretti exhaled, her voice low. "Alright. Probably best to get moving anyway."

She turned the key.

The engine rumbled to life. Just as she dropped it into gear, a scream ripped through the night. It wasn't human, but close enough to make her blood go cold. High and broken, like a woman dying a slow, torturous death.

The rear tires spun.

Jacobi flicked his eyes toward the back window, then down at the dash. "Why the hell aren't we moving?"

Beretti frowned, adjusting her grip. "I think we're caught on something."

She tapped the camera feed on the dash. A log, thick, freshly placed, sat wedged against the right rear tire.

Jacobi stared. "What the hell? I didn't see that before. Didn't hear it either. How did they get that close?"

"I can jump out and pull it," Jacobi added.

She snapped her head toward him. "No. No way. You open that door and they'll grab you before your boots hit the dirt."

A loud slap hit the rear quarter panel. Then another. And another. Like fists slamming flat against metal.

They both froze.

More slaps. Dozens now. The SUV shook with the force of it. It sounded like a hailstorm, only angrier. Faster. Heavy impacts from every angle except the front. The windows held. The body groaned.

Beretti feathered the throttle, then again, trying to rock the vehicle back and forth. The tires skidded, caught, skidded again.

She gripped the wheel tighter and gave it more gas. The

SUV lurched, slipped again. One wheel finally bounced over the log but got snagged on the angle. She braked, backed up a hair, angled the tires again.

The rocks hitting the SUV got louder. Heavier. A thunk rattled the roof.

"Go!" Jacobi said, his voice edged with urgency.

Beretti floored it and the rear tires finally popped free. The log spun aside with a crunch as they tore out and back onto the road.

Jacobi looked behind them, breathing fast. "You see any of them?"

Beretti shook her head, hands still locked on the wheel. "No. Probably a good thing."

Neither of them spoke again until they were halfway back to town.

The forest didn't give up its secrets. But it didn't need to.

They already knew what was out there.

And now it knew them too.

CHAPTER 37

The SUV pulled up outside Ben's place just after four in the morning. The sky hadn't begun to change yet, but the chill in the air hinted that sunrise wasn't far off. Frost clung to the grass along the drive, silvering the tips of the hedges and the front steps.

Beretti parked at the edge of the road, just far enough to keep the headlights from shining into the windows. She shut off the engine and sat back.

Jacobi gave her a look. "We going in?"

Beretti shook her head. "Not yet. The dogs'll hear us and raise hell. That'll wake Leoni and Ben. Let them sleep."

Jacobi didn't argue. He leaned his head back against the seat, eyes half-lidded. "Guess we're napping in style tonight."

Beretti offered a tired smirk, then adjusted her seat and

settled in. They sat in silence, the cab of the SUV growing colder as the engine cooled. The air outside felt paused, like the world itself hadn't quite decided to begin the new day.

They drifted in and out of light sleep until the horizon softened from black to blue.

By the time they stepped inside, the kitchen lights were already on and the smell of coffee floated out to meet them.

Whiskey and Wink greeted them like royalty had returned. Beretti crouched and rubbed Whiskey's ears while Wink danced in place, one-eyed and eager. They barked once, sharp and short, and then were satisfied.

Leoni appeared from the hallway, hair tucked under a knit cap, coffee in one hand.

"You look like hell," she said, not unkindly. "Go shower. I'll keep your coffee hot."

Jacobi turned to Beretti. "You want to go first?"

She shook her head. "Nah. Go ahead. I'll go next."

Jacobi didn't argue. He disappeared down the hall with a grateful nod.

Beretti hung her coat and leaned against the counter,

watching the coffee drip into the pot. Leoni poured her a mug before she could ask.

"Milk's in the fridge. Toast's on the counter. Help yourself. "I've gotta take these two sleepyheads outside." Leoni said as the dogs trotted behind her to the back door.

"Thanks." Beretti replied.

Ben came down the hall dressed in uniform, already looking like he'd been up an hour. He grabbed a piece of toast on his way through the kitchen.

"I'll check in with dispatch. Be back later."

Beretti gave him a quick nod. "Be safe."

He lifted the toast in a silent salute and ducked out the door.

By the time Jacobi returned, hair damp and clothes fresh, Beretti had poured herself a second cup and was halfway through her toast. She stood, handed him the rest of the coffee, and made her way to the shower without a word.

Fifteen minutes later, they sat at the kitchen table looking a little more human. Leoni dropped two plates in front of them, scrambled eggs, toast and a few leftover roasted vegetables from the night before.

"Eat. Then figure out what the hell you two are doing with yourselves."

They didn't talk much over breakfast. The night's tension still lingered, a residue neither of them had words for yet.

When Beretti pushed her plate back, she glanced toward the door.

"I've got an errand to run."

Jacobi looked up. "Want company?"

She hesitated. "It's just a thing I need to check out."

He didn't press. "Alright."

A pause. Then she sighed, gave him a half-smile. "You can come. But you're buying lunch."

"Deal."

They placed their dishes in the sink, grabbed their coats, and stepped out into the soft morning light. Frost still lingered on the grass, and the wind carried the scent of damp earth and lingering ash from a nearby chimney.

They didn't talk as they got into the SUV. They were comfortable enough not to fill the silence with pointless conversation.

Beretti started the engine and pulled out slowly.

This errand wasn't just a drive.

She hadn't said where they were going.

But Jacobi had a feeling he'd find out soon enough.

CHAPTER 38

The town of Blackridge moved through its morning like it always had: quiet, unhurried, and blissfully unaware.

Beretti drove with one hand on the wheel, eyes fixed ahead as the SUV rolled through the heart of town. On the sidewalks, locals bundled in layers strolled with dogs on leashes. A mother adjusted a scarf around her daughter's chin outside the bakery. A teenager zipped by on an e-bike, earphones in his ears.

It looked peaceful. Normal.

But Jacobi knew better. So did Beretti.

They passed the old feed store with the sagging awning, then the rust-red post office. Beretti made a slow right onto Black Crow Lane, and Jacobi noticed something change in her.

Her expression flattened. Shoulders squared. Eyes

narrowed just slightly, like she was staring down a path she didn't want to walk.

He didn't comment. Just watched the quiet shift settle into her posture.

About a mile up, she slowed and turned into a narrow driveway. The house that came into view looked like it had been resting for a very long time.

It was a low-slung, single-story farmhouse with faded white siding and dark gray trim. The lawn surrounding it was surprisingly well-kept, mowed back in a wide circle that reached roughly forty yards in every direction. Beyond that, the grass grew longer, gradually giving way to tree line and bramble at the edges. A few garden beds hugged the front of the house, nothing elaborate, but tidy. The concrete path leading to the porch was swept clean.

Beretti parked and killed the engine.

Jacobi looked toward the house. "Friend or family?"

"Neither," she said. "Old neighbor of mine."

She reached for the door handle, then paused. "Tania cornered me in the bathroom last night at IronHowl."

Jacobi looked over. "Yeah? What'd she want?"

"She said a lot of things. But one of them was that if I wanted the truth, I should come see Ole Man Richards."

Jacobi frowned. "What does that mean?"

Beretti opened her door. "I guess we're about to find out."

They stepped out as a bird called once from somewhere in the trees, but otherwise the world around them was still.

Beretti knocked twice on the screen door.

It creaked slightly under the weight of her hand.

A moment later, the screen door creaked slightly as the interior door behind it swung open with a long moan from its hinges.

A man stood just inside, seventy, maybe older. Tall but slightly hunched, with a narrow face and sharp eyes set deep beneath thick white brows. His jaw hadn't seen a razor in days, and a wool cardigan hung loosely from his shoulders.

He peered at them without blinking. "What can I do for you folks?"

Beretti straightened. "Mr. Richards? My name is Nicole.

This is FBI Special Agent Jacobi. We're working with the sheriff's office, looking into some unusual predator sightings in the area. Would you mind if we came in for a quick word?"

The old man studied her for a long second. His eyes settled on hers, long enough that Jacobi thought he might close the door without another word.

But finally, Richards stepped back and swung the screen door wider. "Come in. It'd be nice to have some company."

The interior was simple, clean, even comforting. The carpet was a worn mustard color, the furniture a faded brown floral, probably from the early seventies. Everything was in its place. Not a newspaper or mug out of order.

An old television buzzed quietly in the far corner, its color faded and edges curved. On the screen, the cast of *The Golden Girls* shared a laugh. A woman sat in a recliner facing it, motionless except for the slight twitch of one hand. She didn't look their way.

"My wife, Dora," Richards said as he gestured them inside. "She's not ignoring you. Just doesn't really leave that show anymore. Dementia's been gettin' worse this past year. But that program, she still laughs at it."

"I'm sorry to hear that," Jacobi said quietly.

Richards nodded like he'd heard it plenty. "Would you two like some water? Coffee?"

"No, thank you," Beretti said.

He moved with slow, careful steps, settling into the recliner opposite his wife's. He gestured for them to take the couch.

"Apologies. Name's Edwin Richards, though most around here just call me Ole Man Richards. Habit, I guess. Been here long enough."

Jacobi smiled politely. "Appreciate you letting us in, sir."

Richards waved it off. "You're with this pretty lady. You're alright."

Beretti sat forward slightly. "We're tracking a few incidents around the outskirts of town. Animals taken, a couple of attacks. We've been asking around. Thought maybe you'd heard or seen anything strange lately."

Richards scratched his chin. "Can't say I have. Not directly. I don't go out much these days. Not since Dora took the turn. Got a nurse that comes a few times a week, food delivery every third day. I fetch the mail. That's about it."

Beretti nodded. "How long have you lived here?"

He chuckled. "Whole life. Born just down the ridge. This house belonged to my grandfather. He passed it to my folks, and then to me. Same soil. Same walls."

Beretti leaned back a little. "Ever seen anything... unusual? In the woods? Creatures that aren't exactly normal?"

Richards arched a brow. "Well now. That depends on what your version of 'unusual' is."

Beretti gave a small chuckle. "Let's say larger than a bear. Smarter than a cat."

The old man tilted his head, eyes narrowing. "You talkin' about the Hairy Man?"

Jacobi raised his eyebrows slightly. Beretti didn't move.

"Yes," she said.

Richards nodded once, like he'd expected it. "They've been here longer than we have."

"You've seen them?" Beretti asked.

He shifted in his chair and looked between them. "You

want the long or the short of it?"

Beretti didn't hesitate. "The long, please."

"Alright then. Get comfortable." He leaned back slightly, hand resting on the arm of the chair. "First time I was 'bout sixteen. Me and a buddy were huntin' out back. That'd be the south stretch, forty acres or so. Still dark when we went out. Had our gear. Walked the edge of the creek line. Something started movin' with us. Not on four legs. On two. Kept pace, just out of sight."

Jacobi sat forward, listening.

Richards continued, voice low and calm. "We made it to the tree stands. Sat up there for hours. No deer. No squirrels. Even the bugs shut up. But we kept hearin' owl calls. Same pattern. Too perfect."

He scratched his knee absently. "By midday we gave up. Climbed down, started back. Soon as we hit the trail, it followed us again. My buddy Joe spun around and caught a glimpse of it. Said he saw its head peek from the brush. Big, dark face. Tall. Eyes like coals."

"What did you do?" Jacobi asked.

"Ran. Like we'd lit a fire under our boots. Heard it

followin' us. Big steps. Too darn big."

He pointed to the floor. "Burst through that door like the devil was chasin' us. My mother was in the kitchen. She just nodded and said, 'Told you not to mess with the Hairy Man.' Never doubted her again."

Beretti tilted her head. "You've seen more since?"

"A few. Mostly glimpses at the tree line. Heard them plenty though. They knock on trees, holler like someone dyin'. But they never hurt us. Not once. Not even when they came close to the house. Used to leave apples on the edge of the yard sometimes. They'd take them. Never left a mess. Always careful."

He paused.

"But then Red Eyes showed up."

Beretti didn't hide the shift in her tone. "Who was Red Eyes?"

Richards's face darkened. The light from the window caught the lines on his jaw, deep and worn.

"Ugliest and meanest creature I ever laid eyes on," he said. "Saw it twice. Never want to again."

Jacobi leaned forward. "Can you describe it?"

Richards hesitated. "Alright."

"Chestnut hair. Not like the others. Long and thick. Two streaks of silver down the back of its head like someone painted it. Bigger than the rest. At least nine feet tall, maybe ten. Arms like tree trunks. Built like *William "The Refrigerator" Perry* was glued together three times."

He glanced between them, then sat back a little, like the memory had crept up from somewhere he'd tried to bury.

"First time was back in… oh-two, I think. I was drivin' home from town with Dora. Took the scenic route because she always loved that stretch. We were headin' down that gravel road west of the creek, just as the light was startin' to fade. I saw movement out in the field and figured it was just a deer."

He swallowed, the memory close enough to shadow his features.

"But then the darn thing stood up."

"It moved as if it had no bones, rising up from the earth in one smooth motion. I slowed the truck. Looked right at it. Thing turned its head and just stared. And its face… Lord. It looked unnatural. As if it was made by someone who had only heard a description of a face but never seen one."

He gave a shiver and rubbed his arm. "Then it did something I'll never forget. It smiled, or maybe snarled. I couldn't tell. But its face contorted, twisted into somethin' so ugly I had nightmares for months. My Dora screamed, and I hit the gas."

He fell quiet.

Jacobi and Beretti didn't speak. The air in the room felt denser somehow.

Finally, Richards looked at them again. His voice had gone softer as he shot a quick look over at Dora.

"That was the first time. The second..."

He let out a long sigh and rubbed his face with one hand.

"That was about twenty years ago when Red Eyes killed the couple up the road. They had the same last name as the sheriff..." He paused, thinking. "Beretti."

THE STORY CONTINUES IN PART TWO.

ABOUT THE AUTHOR

 Luka T. Jacobs, an author from the picturesque Illawarra region south of Sydney, Australia, is passionate about cryptids like Sasquatch and Dogman. She lives there with her partner and their dog, Finnigan.

Luka's love for animals and adventure fuels her storytelling. With a background in Graphic Design and Art, she adds a unique visual flair to her work. An avid traveler and explorer, she draws inspiration from the wild, eager to share her imaginative worlds with readers.

Luka T. Jacobs

Stay connected and join the conversation! *Follow me on **Facebook** to interact and share your thoughts, explore my books on Amazon, and visit my website for more information about my works and upcoming releases. Don't forget to sign up for my newsletter—you'll be the first to hear about new books, exclusive content and special offers!*

FB: https://www.facebook.com/lukatjacobs
A: https://amazon.com/author/lukatjacobs
W: http://www.LukaTJacobs.com

JOIN CRYPTID HORROR CENTRAL

Join my email list and get first access to new releases and download my **FREE** short story *"The Dogman of Coldwater Creek"*.

WWW.LUKATJACOBS.COM

Dear Reader,

Thank you for diving into my book amidst a sea of choices, it truly means the world to me.

If you enjoyed the story, I'd love it if you shared your experience with others and left a review. As an independent author, your voice helps bring these tales to life for more readers, and every recommendation makes a tremendous impact.

Thank you again for joining me on this journey. I'm so grateful to have you as a reader!